ZULU
DOG

ZULU DOG

ANTON FERREIRA

FRANCES FOSTER BOOKS · FARRAR, STRAUS AND GIROUX
NEW YORK

Copyright © 2002 by Anton Ferreira
All rights reserved
Distributed in Canada by Douglas & McIntyre Ltd.
Printed in the United States of America
Designed by Robbin Gourley
First edition, 2002
3   5   7   9   10   8   6   4   2

Library of Congress Cataloging-in-Publication Data
Ferreira, Anton.
    Zulu dog / Anton Ferreira.
        p.   cm.
    Summary: In post-apartheid South Africa, a Zulu boy keeps secrets from his
family as he cares for an injured dog and befriends the daughter of a
white farmer.
    ISBN 0-374-39223-4
    [1. Dogs—Fiction.   2. Friendship—Fiction.   3. Race relations—South
Africa—Fiction.   4. Zulu (African people)—Fiction.   5. South Africa—
Fiction.]   I. Title.

PZ7.F366 Zu 2002
[Fic]—dc21

                                                    2001050156

IN MEMORY OF
MY MOTHER, ROSA

ACKNOWLEDGMENTS

I would probably never have written this book if Sian Hall had not introduced me to my own Zulu dog, Shumba. Shumba in turn led me to Vera Drummond, who showed us both how much fun dog training can be, and to Kevin Behan, who planted the seed for the book in my mind. My agent, Joan Raines, provided welcome encouragement and guidance, and Frances Foster was the best editor a writer could wish for. Rian Malan generously shared his excellent storytelling skills, and I'm deeply grateful to Creina Alcock for her hospitality in Msinga. And heartfelt thanks to my wife, Lynn, for everything.

South Africa's history is largely written in blood, blood that has been shed during centuries of warfare over grazing land, gold, diamonds, and ethnic differences. The country's wide-open prairies and mines have drawn migrants from across the world, but South Africa never became a melting pot; it is more like a witch's cauldron.

The settlers who arrived from the Netherlands, France, and Germany about 350 years ago hunted the original hunter-gatherer inhabitants like vermin and drove them close to extinction. The descendants of these settlers became known as the Afrikaners, and as they pushed north into the interior, they found themselves on a collision course with pastoralist African tribes such as the Zulus who were moving south.

The Afrikaners regarded the blacks, who had no written language, dressed in animal hides, and still fought with sticks and spears, as inferior, heathen savages. In the ensuing wars of conquest, the whites, though vastly outnumbered, gradually came to dominate the region through force of arms. The Afrikaners attributed their victories to God, and many of them interpreted the Bible as decreeing that whites should maintain their racial purity and should rule over blacks.

The wars were fought not only between black and

white—black tribes fought each other, and the Afrikaners fought and lost a bitter war against the Britons who
flocked to South Africa during the nineteenth century
and eventually declared the whole country a British
colony. Some of the fiercest battles fought by the
British invaders were against Zulu warriors in the eastern province now known as KwaZulu-Natal: *KwaZulu*
means "Place of the Zulus."

During the last century, South Africa's white rulers
denied blacks the right to vote, condemning them to
servitude and imposing the policies known as apartheid—"separateness"—that claimed nearly 90 percent
of the land for whites and forced blacks into over-
crowded, eroded pockets of territory. Racial intermar-
riage was banned, schools were racially segregated, and
blacks could not ride on white buses—they could not
even sit on white park benches.

Black resentment against white minority rule led to
the creation of groups like the African National Congress (ANC), whose leader, Nelson Mandela, was jailed
for life in the early 1960s for advocating armed revolt.
Not all whites supported repression; many voted
against apartheid, and some joined the ANC. In the
1970s and 1980s, black resistance to white rule increased—guerrillas set off car bombs, and students ri-
oted in the streets. Initially the white government held

firm, citing the anarchy and chaos in black-ruled countries to the north as evidence of why the ANC could not be allowed to prevail. Given the chance, South Africa's blacks would drive the whites from the country, the apartheid government predicted, arguing that the Afrikaners had as much right to the land as the Zulus or any other tribe.

But disgust at apartheid drove many countries to impose economic sanctions on South Africa, and in 1990 the white government accepted that it had to scrap the system. Mandela was released from jail, and in 1994 the country held its first all-race election in which the ANC was swept to power.

Did everyone live happily ever after? No. The decades of armed struggle meant the country was awash in weapons, which now ended up in the hands of criminals. Human life came to be regarded as cheap, expendable. The poverty endured by most blacks provided abundant incentives for robbery. The police, who had been responsible for the harsh implementation of apartheid, were held in contempt.

The story that follows is based on the lives of Zulus and whites in post-apartheid South Africa, people who have been shaped by generations of conflict. Some harbor deep hatred; others are trying to overcome the past and build a better future.

ZULU
DOG

CHAPTER

I

THERE IS NO BETTER TIME to be alive than in the hour before dawn in Msinga, when a full moon lights the raw African landscape of craggy hills, flat-topped thorn trees, and flowing water in the heart of ancient Zululand. Later the fierce midday sun of early January will bake the rocks here along the banks of the Tugela River, driving man and beast into the shade of the acacia trees, but now the air is cool and invigorating. The star-filled southern sky dazzles this part of the earth where no city lights cast their glare. The night pulses with the lives of nocturnal creatures—a giant eagle owl hoots from the tall trees along the river, and a sudden bawl of alarm echoes across the valley from a distant tribe of baboons woken by a prowling leopard.

A dozen mud-and-thatch huts are grouped on the bank of the river, the kraal of the Ngugu clan, who trace their roots back to Shaka, the legendary warrior king who forged the Zulu nation in eastern South Africa nearly two centuries ago. Clan patriarch Walter Ngugu is snoring, his two-hundred-twenty-pound frame rising and falling gently under the blankets. The whole family is still asleep, but outside, just beyond the treeline at the edge of the kraal clearing, something is stirring in a burrow dug years ago by a porcupine and then abandoned.

Sheba, one of the kraal dogs, crept into the hole the previous evening, heavily pregnant and driven by instinct to find a safe, isolated lair. All night she circled and turned impatiently in the confines of the burrow, scrabbling at the walls to make more room and spreading the sand to form a bed. Now, with the sky lightening in the east, she is ready.

TEN DAYS AFTER THE BIRTH of the puppies, Walter Ngugu's eleven-year-old son, Vusi, is putting the finishing touches to a toy he is making for himself. His brow is furrowed in concentration as he bends bits of discarded wire coat hangers this way and that. He has been working on it for days, and now the toy is all but complete: a scaled-down version of the taxi van his father drives every day to earn a living for the family, about twenty inches long and half as wide. Vusi has shaped wire strands to define the boxy shape of the van, securely fastening the framework to axles fixed to the metal lids of old jars that spin like real wheels. Each joint in the wire skeleton has been painstakingly made so the toy is sturdy enough to withstand the bumps and ruts of the kraal clearing. The final touch is a long piece of wire that stretches from the driver's position and ends in a circle—the steering wheel. Vusi grasps the wheel and triumphantly runs around the kraal, pushing the toy taxi before him as he yells at the top of his lungs.

"Coming through! Coming through! Brrrrrrm brrrrrrm, wake up, old man! We haven't got all day! Out my way, out my way! Beeeeep, beeeeeep!"

Vusi makes a turn at the edge of the clearing, then catches sight of a movement in the bush. He drops the steering wheel and goes to investigate, moving carefully because the long grass is full of snakes and other lurking dangers. The spot where he saw the movement is empty, but he notices tracks in the sand. He snorts in disappointment—just a dog. He follows the track anyway, practicing what his father has taught him in preparation for the day when he becomes a man and must prove himself as a hunter.

Within fifteen yards Vusi comes upon a porcupine burrow, with a series of dog tracks leading in and out. He sinks to his hands and knees and listens with his ear at the opening. He hears the low murmuring squeal of the puppies as they jostle each other, waiting hungrily for the return of their mother. Vusi lies on his stomach and stretches his arm into the hole as far as it will go until his fingers connect with soft fur. He grabs the squirming bundle and pulls it out.

Half a dozen dogs live in and around the kraal, but this is the first time Vusi has seen a newborn puppy. Its eyes are barely open, and its fawn skin seems far too loose for its pudgy body. It grabs Vusi's finger in its tiny mouth and sucks, hoping it has found a teat. Vusi shrieks with joy and runs back to the clearing with the puppy, his toy taxi temporarily forgotten. He puts the puppy down and watches it struggle to its feet, then stagger toward him. He steps backward, and the puppy lurches after him. Vusi picks the puppy up again, cradling it in his arms.

"Vusi!" There is an impatient edge to his mother's voice as it echoes across the clearing, an edge that means there are many chores that need doing. Vusi grabs the puppy in both hands and runs to where his mother is preparing the midday meal.

"Mama, Mama, look what I found!"

Prudence Ngugu's eyes open wide in horror as she sees what her son is thrusting up at her.

"Rubbish! Throw it in the bush! Those things are dirty, Vusi, full of germs, and you want to bring it here where we are making food! Where do you learn such nonsense? Never touch a dog! Take it away, then come back here and eat. But wash yourself first, very carefully."

Abashed, Vusi walks away with the puppy, back to the hole where he found it. He leaves it at the edge of the burrow, then backs off a few paces to see what it will do. The puppy sits down and squeals in despair, thrusting its nose in the air to try to find a familiar smell. As Vusi watches, Sheba emerges from the burrow, throws the boy a quick look, seizes the puppy in her jaws, and returns with it into the den.

CHASTENED BY HIS MOTHER'S DISDAIN for the puppy, Vusi initially resists the temptation to go back to the burrow to play with it again, to feel its soft fur under his hands and offer it a finger to suck on as it squirms in his grasp. His mother's anger is a powerful force, and he has no wish to provoke it. But as the days pass, Vusi's curiosity about Sheba's den grows stronger. His mind wanders off during his school lessons, and when he is home, his games seem to take him closer and closer to the burrow. At last, he can no longer resist the urge to play with them again. If I just go over and take one quick look, it can't do any harm, he tells himself.

So one day when his mother is out collecting firewood, Vusi saunters out of the clearing and into the bush, whistling casually in a way that he hopes will give anyone watching him the impression he has nothing at all on his mind. Once in the cover of the trees, he stealthily works his way around to where the puppies are. Arriving at the hole, he lies down to reach into the den. But as he does so, Sheba gives a low warning growl from the depths. Vusi sits back and considers this. He hadn't thought she might be there, and he doesn't want to have his hand bitten. His mother has warned him that a dog bite means certain death from rabies.

A solution occurs to him. He runs to the kitchen hut, checks to be sure no one is around, and opens the black cast-iron pot full of the stiff corn porridge that is the Zulu staple food. He digs out a handful, dips it in a pan of meat gravy standing nearby, and dashes back to the burrow. Squatting at the entrance, he waves the food around to tempt Sheba with the smell. She quickly slinks out of the hole, her caution overcome by an empty stomach, holding her head low in submission, her tail curled between her legs. Vusi scatters the porridge on the ground, and the dog snatches up the lumps as if she has not eaten for a week. She hardly bothers to chew the pieces before swallowing.

Vusi sees her hunger, and the way her ribs push through her skin, but thinks nothing of it. Kraal dogs are always hungry.

Sheba, one of the best hunters among the Ngugu family's dogs, sniffs the ground for any remaining crumbs of porridge. While she is preoccupied with scavenging, Vusi turns to the porcupine burrow to pull out the puppy. But there is no need—the four puppies have scrambled by themselves up to the lip of the burrow, where they peer around for their mother. Vusi recognizes the one he played with before because it is the only brown one. Two are brindle, and one is white with large brown patches. He lifts his puppy up to his chest to cradle it as he has seen the women do with their babies. Then he holds the puppy at eye level and gazes at it.

"What are you called?" he asks it. The puppy wriggles and licks at Vusi's hands. Tiny teeth emerge from its gums like ivory needle points, and Vusi eases his little finger into the puppy's mouth to feel how sharp they are. The puppy closes its mouth on his finger, and Vusi gasps in surprise at the pain.

As he sucks at the pinprick of blood, Vusi recalls the last time he tested something for sharpness, when he ran a finger across his father's razor blade. He cut himself that time, too.

"Gillette," he announces. "That is your name. Gillette."

Over the next weeks Vusi plays with Gillette every day, being careful not to let the adults see him. The puppies are increasingly independent of their mother, and Sheba quickly comes to accept Vusi's presence at the den. The boy still brings her food, though, because he realizes she needs to keep her strength up while nursing the litter. He cuts reeds down at the river, then weaves them into a seat in his toy taxi so he can put the puppy in the toy and push it up and down the paths through the bush. Twice a day he searches Gillette for ticks, which infest all the kraal dogs. He gently rolls the puppy on its back, carefully pulling off the parasites so their heads do not remain embedded in the skin to fester and spread infection. To end the grooming session, Vusi sends Gillette into a blissful doze by softly rubbing the puppy's tummy.

LIFE UNFOLDS SLOWLY on a Sunday in the Ngugu kraal. As the first soft yellow light brightens the treetops, the rooster that ranges freely around the yard during the day with his harem of hens lifts his head and crows, but uncertainly, as if he is not sure that dawn really has broken or if he is just dreaming it. His call quickly fades to a volley of bad-tempered clucking, then he puts his head under his wing and goes back to sleep. The hens around him ruffle their feathers and shift their weight from foot to foot on their perches, but they don't bother to wake up.

The rooster's gargling call stirs Beauty, a young female dog stretched out on her side on the hard-packed dirt of the kraal clearing. She opens an eye, notices light in the sky above, and slowly rises to her feet, the stiffness of the night still tight in her joints. She yawns, looks around, sees that nothing is moving, then stretches long and slowly, her front paws pushed straight out in front, her haunches up in the air. She holds the stretch, then reverses it, pushing her front legs vertical, craning her twitching nostrils toward the smells of the bush and flexing her rump down toward the ground. Beauty gives a final shake and pads over to where one of the other dogs, Lightning, is lying and collapses on the ground next to him. Lightning, a lithe, brown male dog, twitches in his sleep but does not wake.

The other male dog of the pack, Spear, is curled up some distance away. Spear, Lightning, and Beauty all resemble Sheba with their slim, whippetlike builds, but the fourth dog, Charcoal, sleeping now with one paw over her nose, is smaller and stockier. Pitch-black but for a white blaze on her throat, she is barrel-chested with a blunt muzzle, as if she had Staffordshire terrier blood in her.

Charcoal lifts her nose and sniffs the wind, catching the faint scent of antelope moving through the bush. But her senses tell her the impalas are far off and moving away. They never come close enough to the kraal to make it worthwhile for the dogs to try to catch them. She gets to her feet, shakes herself, and walks over to the remains of last night's fire.

When the weather is clear, the Ngugus eat dinner outdoors, under the stars, sitting on thick tree trunks around the cooking fire. Charcoal sniffs around the tree trunks for dropped food and finds nothing. But closer to the cold ashes, she is rewarded with a charred bone. She grabs it and trots off to a spot far from the other dogs, so they will not try to take it from her.

She's not afraid of Spear or Beauty, but Lightning would challenge her for the bone and attack her if she refused to give it up.

Charcoal chooses to lie with her bone behind a hut at one side of the clearing, near the trees ringing the perimeter of the kraal and some way from the other huts that circle the cooking fire. This is the hut of Grandmother Ngugu. If she has another name, no one ever uses it; she is always "Granny" or "the old woman," uttered in tones of solemn respect.

She is the first of the Ngugus awake this morning, as usual. For her, there is no difference between Sunday and any other day of the week. She has a routine, and she likes to stick to it.

She leans on a stick as she hobbles to the kitchen hut, then bangs pots and pans as she rummages for the kettle. She takes the remaining five pieces of wood from a pile near the door, stacks them in the wood stove, and lights them with trembling fingers. She fills the kettle with water and puts it on the cast-iron stove, grumbling all the while that there is probably not enough wood in the firebox to boil the water for her coffee. Her eyes are no longer sharp, and the dark interior of the kitchen hut makes it hard for her to see. She peers around carefully, to check if there is a stash of firewood that she has missed. But there is none. It was all burned on the fire last night, and no one bothered to cut more.

The old woman picks up a long metal spoon and a frying pan and makes her way stiffly to the hut Vusi and his three sisters share. She pushes open the door, made from salvaged planks of different shapes and sizes, leans against the doorway for support, and clangs the spoon against the frying pan.

"Wake up! Wake up!" the old woman says. "It's late! Why are you all still in bed?" Cries of protest greet the racket.

"Granny, it's Sunday," says Lindiwe, Vusi's sister, who is thirteen and two years older than he. Vusi and Lindiwe share the hut with their twin sisters, Mandisa and Tendeka, who are eight. "We don't go to school today," Mandisa mumbles groggily. "We can sleep late."

"No, no, you must get up. Come on. There is no firewood. You must go and get some. Come, come, quickly." Grandmother Ngugu clangs the frying pan again for emphasis.

The children mutter and groan, but it's no use trying to go back to sleep. Reluctantly they climb out of their beds, their eyes still heavy with sleep, and pull on their clothes.

BY THE TIME THEY RETURN to the kraal, loaded down with dead branches they have found in the bush, the rest of the family is stirring. Their elder brother, Petrus, who is nineteen, is doing stretching exercises, barefoot and dressed only in shorts. Because he has entered manhood and will soon be looking for a wife, he has a hut to himself.

With his limbs sufficiently loose, Petrus picks up his *kierie*—a stick about four feet long, with a knob carved at one end—and starts practicing his stick-fighting moves. He raises his right foot straight out in front of him so his leg is almost parallel with the ground, then swings it in fast and stamps it in the dirt, sending a tremor through the ground that the children can feel where they stand twenty yards away. He grunts a challenge to an imaginary opponent and repeats the kick with his left foot, scattering dust. The shock waves from the impact of his feet slamming into the ground travel up his body and send quivers across his flat abdomen and the muscles of his broad chest. Sweat glints on his black skin.

The younger children watch in awe as Petrus jumps, somersaults, and strikes his invisible rival with his *kierie*. He is performing a stylized dance derived from the way the ancient Zulus used to settle their differences: by fighting it out with sticks.

"Harder! Faster! Higher!" Walter Ngugu shouts encouragement from the doorway of his hut, where he stands bare-chested, contentedly rubbing his vast paunch, contemplating the morning and his son's stick-fighting skills.

"Lindiwe! Vusi!" The voice of their mother echoes across the clearing from the kitchen hut. "Where's that wood? Come, come, bring it here now! We must cook."

BY THE TIME THE SUN has risen above the trees, thick corn porridge is bubbling in an iron pot set on three legs directly over the coals of the open-air fireplace. Sausages are sizzling on a grill nearby. Walter Ngugu is sparring with Petrus, feinting with his stick, exclaiming in triumph when he catches his son off balance. Each holds an ox-hide shield on his left arm, using it to parry the blows of the other. The clearing rings with their grunts of exertion and the thump of stick on shield as the combatants circle each other, sweat pouring off them as they maneuver for advantage under a cloudless sky.

"Warriors! Good day to you!"

Walter and Petrus let their sticks and shields fall to their sides as they turn to greet the visitor, a tall, thin man with a wispy gray beard who leans on a staff cut from an acacia tree.

"Shakes! Welcome my friend!" Walter steps forward to greet his visitor. "Just in time for brunch. Come and sit down here by the fire. Lindiwe! Bring us beer!"

Shakes eases himself down onto one of the logs and turns to Petrus. "I see you are a promising stick fighter. Maybe one day you will be as good as your father. He was the best in Msinga, when he was a young man."

"I still am! I still am! Here, have some beer." Walter hands his guest a mug of homemade sorghum beer, thick and sour, that Lindiwe has brought in a hollowed out calabash.

"So, Shakes, we haven't seen you in months. How have you been?"

"I am well, I am well. Still living here." He gestures downriver.

"How is the hunting?" Walter asks, and adds in an aside to Petrus: "Shakes is the best hunter in Msinga."

Petrus nods and smiles. "Yes, that's what everyone says."

"Well, I had bad luck with my dogs."

"What bad luck, Shakes?"

"You know I had four dogs, very good dogs. But two months ago they all got sick. They were vomiting, they had diarrhea. Two of them were very ill, they were trembling, then they died."

"This is bad," says Walter, shaking his head in sympathy. "And the other two?"

"They're still weak. They get tired very easily. I don't know, maybe they will also die soon. I think they ate poisoned meat somewhere. Some of the farmers around here are putting out poison—you know they hate our dogs."

Shakes's face is tired, sad. "So that's why I've come today, Walter. I need a new dog, and they say one of your dogs is pregnant."

"Yes, that's right. Sheba. She's an excellent hunter, and her puppies will be good dogs, too. They must have been born by now. Petrus, have you seen them?"

"No, Father. Sheba is still in the bush somewhere. She came to the kraal last week for food, but I haven't seen her again."

Walter turns to Shakes. "The puppies will be ready to sell in, oh, about two months, say, early in April."

"Well, if they are good dogs, I will buy two."

"Sheba is a clever hunter. Her puppies will be a hundred rand each."

"I will give you a hundred and sixty rand for two."

Walter takes a gulp of beer.

"A hundred and eighty rand, because we are friends."

"A hundred and seventy-five."

The two men shake hands on the deal.

"You should sell all the puppies." Prudence Ngugu, arriving with plates and forks for the meal, sounds cross. "And if you got rid of all the dogs, it would be even better."

"Oh, Prudence, leave the dogs alone."

"No really, Walter, you know I don't like those animals. Look at them!" She gestures to where Lightning, Beauty, and Spear are sleeping on the edge of the clearing, stretched out in the sun. "Dirty! Full of disease. If you want them, Shakes, you can take them."

Walter turns to Shakes. "We never talk about dogs here. It always starts an argument."

"Dogs are useful, Ma Ngugu," says Shakes, embarrassed to feel he has somehow been the cause of Prudence's anger. "They help us catch food, they chase away robbers—"

"There is no game left around here for them to catch. And what do we have for anyone to steal? A transistor radio with flat batteries. That's all! The chickens are more useful—they give us eggs, and they eat the insects and slugs in the vegetable garden. We should have more chickens and fewer dogs."

"But the dogs don't come near you, Prudence. Just

ignore them." Walter eats his sausage and porridge with gusto. "Also, they eat all the leftover food. They help keep the place clean."

Prudence says no more about the dogs, but as Shakes is leaving two hours later, she tells him: "Shakes, let everyone know that we have lots of dogs for sale. We will even give them away for free."

Vusi almost bursts into tears when he hears this. The younger children have sat silently through the meal, too respectful to interrupt the adults. They have heard the argument about dogs between their parents many times; Vusi knows his mother hates them and his father likes them. He has been hoping that when the time comes, when the future of Sheba's litter is decided, he will be able to talk his father into letting him keep Gillette. Only his father could overrule his mother about the puppies.

But from the angry sound of his mother's voice now, Vusi fears that Gillette might soon be taken from him.

SOMETIME PAST MIDNIGHT on a Saturday night six weeks after he found Gillette, Vusi is woken by a piercing howl, ending abruptly in midnote. It comes from the trees just beyond the kraal clearing, the direction of Sheba's den. It is followed by scuffling sounds, as though the spirits of the bush are fighting. All the dogs join in with a frantic chorus of barking. From his parents' hut, Walter's voice pierces the cacophony, angrily shouting at the dogs to shut up, then muttering as he goes back to bed. Vusi himself is too scared to stir—his grandmother has fed him dozens of tales of the dangers, seen and unseen, that lurk in the bush at night. The howl sounded like an anguished dog, but it could also have been one of the ghosts his grandmother described. Vusi rolls over, too nervous and worried to go back to sleep.

In the morning he is up before anyone else, his bare feet kicking up sand as he runs across the dew-damp dirt of the clearing to the big yellow-wood tree that stands over the porcupine burrow. He halts in horror at the den. The long grass and bushes have been torn and flattened, as if by a whirlwind. The ground is scuffed, scraped, ripped. Drag marks lead off deeper into the trees. Worse, the earth is stained black with a dark, viscous gel. Blood.

Vusi turns and runs back to the kraal, tears brimming in his eyes.

"Daddy! Daddy!" he yells, bursting into the kitchen hut where his father is cradling the day's first mug of coffee in his callused hands. "Something has happened to Sheba. Something bad, I think."

"What? What are you saying?"

"Come and look. That noise last night—it came from the hole where Sheba was living with her puppies. Something bad has happened there."

Prudence, cooking over the stove, raises her eyebrows but says nothing. Walter frowns, puts down his coffee, and follows Vusi across the clearing and into the trees. When they come to the entrance of the burrow, Walter gives a low whistle. Fresh scars in the earth show where a beast's claws have torn at the entrance.

"Sheba was hiding her puppies here? How do you know?"

"I saw her once. And the puppies, too. There were four of them."

"And you didn't say anything to anyone?"

"I showed one of the puppies to Mother, but she was very angry."

Walter looks around at the signs of struggle in the bush. He sees what looks like a bloody rag on the ground and bends down to pick it up. He studies it quickly, then throws it away into the thicket with a muttered curse. A piece of torn dog skin.

"Leopard. They like to eat dogs." He shakes his head sorrowfully and kneels down next to the hole, listening. He cautiously extends his arm into the burrow and feels around. When he stands again, his mouth is set in a grim line.

"The leopard ate everything. Even the puppies. The hole is empty."

Vusi bows his head. He doesn't want his father to see his tears.

"It's too bad," says Walter. "Sheba was a very good dog, very clever. Her puppies would have been good hunters." He sighs. "There goes my hundred and seventy-five rand from Shakes."

When his father has gone, Vusi falls to the ground at the entrance to the burrow. The boy stretches his hand down the hole and feels nothing but sand. He wants to cry, but he refuses to give up hope. He pushes his shoulder as far as it will go, trying to reach deeper, imagining his arm is an elastic band as he stretches, stretches, stretches. His fingers scrabble furiously in the dirt at the bottom of the hole, hoping for the touch of warm puppy fur. Nothing.

Vusi lets his hand go limp there and surrenders to his sorrow. But as the first deep sobs shake his body, a spark of electricity seems to shoot up his arm from his little finger. He wiggles the finger. It touches something sharp, like a needle. Then something soft, wet, and warm, like the tongue of a puppy.

"Gillette! Gillette!" Joy floods Vusi's being. The

puppy is still too far down the burrow for him to grab it, so he withdraws his hand an inch and wiggles his fingers. The puppy crawls forward and fixes its mouth to a finger. The sharp grip of the puppy's teeth makes Vusi smile.

"Come, Gillette, come," he whispers down the hole. He lures the puppy inch by inch toward the surface, until he can get a grip around its body and pull it up and out of the hole.

Vusi lifts Gillette triumphantly into the air, then freezes. The puppy's right back leg is a mangled, bloody mess, the bottom half hanging by a thread of skin from the thigh. The leopard that carried off Sheba and the other puppies inflicted this terrible wound, too, catching Gillette with a sharp claw as he cowered at the bottom of the burrow. Vusi realizes Gillette will die if he doesn't do something quickly.

When he cuts himself, he goes to his mother, who washes the wound and bandages it. But it is out of the question to take the puppy to her. Clutching Gillette firmly to his chest, Vusi runs to the small hut standing away from the others at the edge of the clearing, under the shade of the forest trees, and kneels at the low doorway.

"Granny?" he asks urgently. "Granny? Are you here?" Vusi's voice catches as he battles to halt the sobs that want to bubble up from his throat. Blood from Gillette's leg is soaking his clothes. If his grandmother cannot help, the puppy will surely bleed to death.

A bony, withered hand grasps the curtain hanging at the hut entrance and pulls it aside. A thin, high voice greets him: "Vusi, what do you want, boy?"

Granny Ngugu, her eyes covered by cataracts, shields her wrinkled face from the glare of the sun as she peers at her visitor and his bloody load. "Come inside, boy, come inside, it's too bright out here."

Vusi seldom visits his grandmother in her hut, not because the old woman does not like visitors, but because the hut sends chills down his spine.

As he enters, he ducks his head to avoid brushing against the objects hanging from the thatched roof. He doesn't mind the bunches of dried herbs and plants, but there are other things, some recognizable, some not, that he doesn't want scraping across his skull as they dangle in the air. There is a shriveled ground squirrel covered in the dust of decades, the sharp tail of a scaly anteater, a set of gray bones clinking softly together like wind chimes, some other creature with moldy whiskers and empty eye sockets, strips of dried animal skin curling in weird spirals, and a baby crocodile whose rows of teeth grimace in a wide, mirthless smile. The walls of the hut are worse: rows of shelves are packed with jars and bottles, many containing slowly disintegrating animal parts. Cold coils of deadly cobras, tree snakes, pythons, and adders float in murky preserving liquid. The lintel above the doorway supports an array of monkey skulls.

Granny Ngugu motions Vusi to sit on her bed, which is raised on bricks to put it above the reach of the evil dwarves that the old woman knows visit her hut when she is asleep. A shy young woman is already sitting there.

"This is Lucy. She has come very far today, many miles. She needs something special to keep her husband close. He likes to roam, that one." Vusi's granny cackles, her mouth wide, showing the only two teeth she has left. "Men! There is always something new to take their fancy. But I am making Lucy a very strong mixture to put in her husband's food. Then he will never look at any other woman ever again. He will only have eyes for her."

Lucy blushes and remains silent, head bowed.

"Granny, please, can you help me? Can you save my puppy?"

He holds out Gillette, who whimpers as the torn stump drips blood onto the dirt floor of the hut. The severed foot still hangs loosely from the thigh by a piece of skin.

The old woman quickly holds out a tin cup to catch the drops. "Young dog's blood, very good, very good," she mutters.

Putting the cup aside, she looks at the puppy, thinks for a minute, and gazes up at her hanging collection of healing and hexing materials. Straightening her crooked back, she stretches up and plucks a selection of dried leaves and herbs. Taking Gillette from Vusi, she quickly slices off the hanging foot with a rusty knife and carefully places it on a shelf behind her. The boy tries not to think what his grandmother is going to use it for later. The old woman binds the herbs and leaves to the stump with a bandage, then dips a finger into a vial of pungent oil. She thrusts the finger into the puppy's mouth and holds it closed so Gillette is forced to swallow. She hands the puppy back to Vusi.

"There. He will be fine."

"Thank you, Granny, thank you." Vusi strokes Gillette's head, careful as he cradles the puppy not to touch the injured leg. "You will not tell my mother, will you? She doesn't like this puppy."

"Don't worry, boy, this puppy is a secret."

FROM HIS GRANNY'S HUT, Vusi dashes to the kitchen. He wants to feed the puppy, but his mother is still standing at the stove. He looks around for a place to hide the whimpering creature and finds a bucket, with sides too high for Gillette to climb. He pulls off his bloodstained shirt and pushes it into the bottom of the bucket. Carefully laying the puppy on this nest, Vusi then grabs a handful of dirt and rubs it into the blood-stains on his shorts, so they look like fresh smears of mud. Some blood has soaked through his shirt onto his torso; he gives it the same camouflage treatment. He enters the kitchen and forces himself to look casual.

"Can I have some breakfast, please, Mother?"

Prudence ladles porridge into a dish for him. "That puppy you showed me. Didn't I tell you to throw it away?"

"I put it back where I found it, Mother, in the bush."

"Well, I'm glad the leopard got it. If the leopard hadn't killed those puppies, I would have killed them myself. We don't need more dogs around here. Smelly, dirty animals, they leave their hair everywhere, they eat too much. They are dangerous. Your father is too kind to them. You must not be like him, Vusi, with dogs. You must leave those things alone."

"Yes, Mother."

For each spoonful of porridge he puts in his mouth, Vusi surreptitiously sneaks a piece into his pocket.

When his plate is clean, he gets up and goes out the door. "I'm going down to the river to fetch water, Mother."

"Good boy. While you're there, give yourself a wash. You've got mud all over you," Prudence says. His offer to fetch water disarms her. She had been thinking there was something suspicious about his meek acceptance of her order to have nothing to do with dogs. But as she watches Vusi walk down toward the river with the bucket, she puts her suspicions out of her mind. He's an obedient boy, she tells herself.

As soon as he gets to the river, concealed from view, Vusi lifts Gillette from the bucket and cradles him to his chest. He breaks off pea-size bits from the lumps of porridge in his pocket and feeds them to the shivering puppy, who is so weak he has to be coaxed to accept them. When the porridge is finished and the puppy's belly is full, his shaking eases, and he falls asleep against Vusi's body.

There is no question now of leaving Gillette by himself in the porcupine burrow at night—but what is he to do with the puppy? His mother would be furious if she learned that Vusi has ignored her orders to get rid of his pet.

Vusi carries Gillette to the hut he shares with

his sisters. All three are inside, doing their homework.

"Sisters, look what I have here."

He lays Gillette on his bed, putting a towel down first in case more blood oozes from the wound.

The girls gather around the bed and squeal in delight. "Where did you find him?" "What's his name?" "Look, he's hurt." "What happened to his leg?"

"Don't pick him up, Tendeka, he's sick. When he's better, you can hold him. He was attacked by a leopard."

His sisters gasp in unison.

"You heard the noise in the bush last night?" The girls nod. "That was the leopard killing his mother and his brothers and sisters."

"Oh, no," the twins gasp. "Poor thing," says Lindiwe. "What are you going to do with him?"

"He is my best friend. I'm going to keep him always. But you must all help me, please."

"If you let me hold him," says Tendeka.

"Yes, but not yet. When he is strong again."

"What do you want us to do?" asks Mandisa.

"Don't tell Mother about him, please, please. That's all. I will keep him here in the hut at night, then every day, first thing in the morning before Mother comes over here, I'll take him out into the bush and hide him. Mother mustn't know about him."

His sisters look aghast, but they promise to keep his secret.

Vusi goes to sleep that night with Gillette curled up against his stomach. He is woken early the next morning by the puppy sucking on his finger, whining softly for food. The boy dresses quickly, gathers up Gillette, and walks through the dawn light to the porcupine burrow. He puts a big lump of porridge softened with milk into the burrow, then eases the puppy into the hole, too. Next he goes over to a heavy rock lying some yards away and heaves it across to the burrow, blocking the entrance so the puppy is trapped inside.

"This is for your own good," he whispers to Gillette. "So you will be safe. I'll be back soon with more food, after school. Goodbye, be well."

Vusi turns and runs back to the kraal for breakfast and to get ready for school.

The stump of the puppy's hind leg heals well. Gillette tears off the bandage and herbal poultice while he is alone in the burrow and spends hours licking the wound clean, the antiseptic action of his own saliva helping his recovery.

Vusi's heart goes out to Gillette as he watches the puppy struggle to learn to walk all over again. Gillette pushes himself upright, then immediately falls over with a yelp of surprise when he tries to put weight on his nonexistent back leg. But within two or three days, the pup masters the art of walking and running on three legs, although Vusi realizes Gillette will never outsprint the other kraal dogs.

"Never mind, Gillette. You are not so fast, but you will be clever, you will be wise." For Vusi has decided that Gillette is going to be the best hunting dog ever seen in Zululand, one of the rare dogs that are remembered long after they die, that become the hero of tales told by the men of the kraal around the fire at night.

All Vusi knows of dog training is what he has learned from watching his father and Petrus with the other dogs. They whistle in a special way and hold out a piece of meat, so the dogs learn to run to the men when they hear that whistle. Apart from that, as far as Vusi can tell, the dogs rely on their own instincts during a hunt. They respond very keenly to his father and brother; if the men shout at them in angry voices, the dogs cower and look miserable; if the men praise them, they wag their tails shyly and pant with their tongues hanging out, looking for all the world as if they are smiling.

Vusi thinks about asking his father and Petrus for advice on training. But he has not told them about

Gillette, fearing that if his father knew one of Sheba's puppies had survived the leopard attack, he might want to sell it to his friend Shakes.

No, Gillette must be my secret. I will train him myself, he decides.

He conducts Gillette's education by relying on his instincts and doing what feels right. The first thing he must teach the dog is to stay in one place. The other kraal dogs can come and go more or less as they please, but because his mother has taken a dislike to this puppy, Gillette has to stay in the bush without running off and getting lost or, just as bad, following Vusi into the kraal and being seen. Until now, the puppy has been content to spend hours on end sleeping in the porcupine burrow while Vusi is at school or doing chores around the kraal, but the boy knows that as Gillette grows more active they will need a new system.

Vusi starts by making Gillette a rope collar, then tying him to a tree near the porcupine burrow. He turns and walks away, wondering what the puppy will do. He quickly finds out: as soon as he disappears from the puppy's sight, Gillette starts howling. Vusi carries on walking for a few minutes, hoping the howling will die down if he ignores it. It doesn't—if anything, it grows louder. He stops, frowning. The howls are so piercing, his mother might hear them and come to investigate. That would be the end of Gillette. Vusi turns and hurries back to where he has tied the puppy. He has barely taken ten paces when suddenly the howling stops. The silence alarms Vusi more than the howling. What has happened? Did the leopard hear the noise, come to investigate, and find the puppy? Vusi starts sprinting back toward the place where he tied Gillette.

As he runs, he hears the sound of something breaking through the undergrowth toward him, but it's too small to be a leopard. Then the bounding puppy, free from his tether, throws himself against Vusi's legs, his tail whipping in delight that he has found Vusi. The boy looks at the rope trailing from Gillette's collar—it has been chewed clean through.

A different approach is needed, Vusi realizes. I must get Gillette to be comfortable staying in one place, convinced that he has not been abandoned, trusting that I will return to him at any moment.

"Lie down," he tells Gillette firmly, holding a piece of porridge on the ground. The puppy drops onto his stomach and nuzzles the hand holding the food. Vusi puts down another piece of porridge, saying, "Stay here," and backs away a couple of paces. Then he immediately returns and places another morsel on the ground in front of Gillette's nose.

Gradually, over days and weeks, Vusi extends the time and the distance before returning with food, until one day he can hide behind a tree for thirty minutes without Gillette budging from the spot where he has been told to stay. Sometimes Gillette sits up and scratches himself, sometimes he stands, yawns, and makes a small circle before lying down again, but he always stays in the same place.

In the months that follow, Vusi spends every free moment with his dog. He watches the puppy closely, trying to figure out ways of communicating to him what he wants him to learn. He sees how quickly Gillette reacts to movement, how excited he gets when the wind blows a fluttering leaf across his path, how he loves to chase and pounce.

Vusi talks to Gillette all the time.

"You're a natural hunter, aren't you, puppy? You know how to chase, how to bite, how to sniff the world around you to find where your prey is. There's nothing I can teach you about that."

Vusi rubs Gillette's loose coat vigorously, ruffling up the short, coarse hairs.

"But you must learn to hunt in a team with me. You must be watching me when we hunt, listening to me. Otherwise you will just be another wild animal."

Vusi's hand closes on a river pebble, rounded

smooth by the action of water. He picks it up, holds it in front of Gillette's face.

"Look!"

Vusi flicks the pebble along the ground, so it rolls through the carpet of noisy dry leaves like a live thing. Gillette leaps after it, lacking coordination still but firmly fixed on the moving pebble. He grasps it in his mouth, finds the hard cold surface unappetizing, and quickly drops it. The puppy looks up at Vusi expectantly.

"You like that game? But a pebble is not nice to bite, is it?" Vusi thinks. His face brightens as the solution occurs to him. "Stay here," he tells the puppy, then runs back to the kraal.

FIFTEEN MINUTES LATER he returns, smiling broadly. Gillette is accustomed to being given food at the end of a stay, so his tail beats in anticipation. But this time it's not food that Vusi is holding in his hand—it's a foot-long piece of antelope hide, an offcut from a belt his father is making.

"Okay," Vusi shouts, issuing the command that releases the puppy from his stay. Vusi waggles the hide in front of Gillette, who lunges at it with flashing teeth but misses. Vusi shakes it on the ground, making it writhe like an angry snake, and Gillette pounces again, trapping an end under his paws. He grabs the skin in his jaws and shakes it, dashes off a few yards, shakes it some more, chews it, then runs around Vusi in circles, stiff-legged, head high, triumphantly dangling his prize from his mouth.

Vusi grabs one end of the hide thong and plays tug-of-war with Gillette. The puppy sets his front paws firmly in the dirt, growls, clamps his teeth tighter, and thrusts backward with his one hind leg. Vusi resists for a couple of minutes, then releases his end of the thong and grins as Gillette carries it off and worries it on the ground as though it were a live creature he has just caught. Vusi lets the puppy play with the thong a bit longer, then pries Gillette's jaw open and takes back the well-chewed hide. He conceals it in his pocket, pleased at how Gillette, his tail wagging vigorously, watches like a hawk to see if the wonderful-smelling prey that feels so good between his teeth will reappear.

"You like that, don't you? You would do anything to get that piece of skin in your mouth, right? I've found the way to train you, and you won't even know you're being trained. It won't be anything like going to school. You'll think you're just having fun!" Vusi tousles Gillette's rough coat. "Okay, a few minutes more playtime."

Vusi takes the thong from his pocket, and the

puppy tenses, eyes wide. The boy tantalizes him, dangling the hide just out of reach.

"Geddit!" he shouts, bringing the thong down low, and Gillette leaps forward, latching onto the hide once more and throwing himself into a new game of tug-of-war.

GILLETTE COMES TO REGARD the strip of hide as the most desirable object under the sun, pawing the ground in excitement and prancing with joy whenever Vusi puts his hand in his pocket. This is the signal that the thong is about to appear and it's time to resume their games. Vusi keeps the games with the thong short, no more than thirty minutes each time, and when they are not playing, he hides the piece of skin from Gillette, so the puppy never begins to get bored with it.

Gradually he develops their games into training exercises. Vusi makes Gillette lie down and wait behind a tree, then he runs off, dragging the skin on the ground, and conceals it in a burrow or in a bush. He runs back to Gillette, tells him "Geddit," and the dog dashes off to find the prize. Sometimes his nose skims along the ground, like a vacuum cleaner, sucking up the scent. Other times Gillette pauses, his head high, sniffing the air. He always finds the skin, even when Vusi increases the distance to more than a hundred yards.

Vusi teaches Gillette everything he thinks will be useful on a hunt—how to be silent, how to run in a straight line following the boy's pointing arm, how to hang on to the piece of skin and not let go, even if Vusi swings him off his legs and into the air. Gillette learns to freeze if Vusi whistles one way, and to run back to him if he whistles a different note. Above all he learns to watch Vusi all the time, to read his body language, to know what the boy wants him to do almost before the boy knows himself.

Vusi knows the story of a hunt that failed because the prey jumped into the river and the dogs refused to swim after it. So he plays with Gillette with a stick, getting the dog to chase it and bring it back. Then he throws the stick into a rock pool by the side of the river—and watches Gillette plunge into the water without hesitation. When he is sure Gillette has no fear of water, Vusi throws the stick into the fast-flowing river itself. Gillette jumps in after it, swimming strongly with his three legs, and snatches the stick from the current. He drags himself onto the bank, gives a shake that sends drops of water flying, and leaps into Vusi's waiting arms.

"Best dog in the world," Vusi tells him. "Best dog in the world."

CHAPTER

2

*F*IVE MILES WEST of the mud-and-thatch huts of the Ngugu kraal stands another homestead, a sprawling collection of angular outbuildings built from steel, concrete, mortar, and brick: a shed for milking cows, a barn for storing hay, a pigpen, and an oversize garage where tractors and other heavy equipment are kept. The natural forest has been cleared for a hundred yards or more in every direction, and in its place are gently sloping pastures kept verdant by irrigation water pumped from the Tugela River. A herd of Angus beef cattle graze the alfalfa, swinging their tails impatiently at biting flies.

The main farmhouse is set away from the outbuildings with their smells and noise, buffered from the rest of the farm and the forest beyond by a well-ordered garden of manicured lawns and rectangular beds filled with roses, carnations, and daisies. Whitewashed rocks line broad gravel paths that cut straight lines between the beds. No weeds grow, and no stone is out of place. If the African wilderness held sway here once, there is no sign of it now. The main garden path leads up wide, polished stone stairs to the generous veranda of the main house, a low, rambling building of spacious rooms linked by long corridors.

IN HER BEDROOM, Shirley Montgomery studies her image in a full-length mirror. Sun-bleached blond hair falls straight to her shoulders, framing pale blue eyes above a light dusting of freckles on her high, tanned cheekbones. It is a young, fresh, open face.

But now it is twisted in a grimace. "Oh, Mother, I'm *not* going to wear this silly dress. It's too—too *cute*. All these bows and frills, and this *color*—this neon pink—I can't possibly wear it. Everyone will laugh at me."

"But Shirley dear, you wore it last year when you were bridesmaid for your cousin Sarah." Shirley's mother, Dorothy Montgomery, thinks her daughter looks adorable in the silk-and-lace dress. Her own mother wore it as a girl, and as a child she often wore it herself on special occasions. For the last week, she has spent hours at her sewing machine, carefully adjusting it to fit her fast-growing daughter.

"Well, last year I was a year younger. I'm twelve now, Mom. I'm not a little girl anymore." Shirley looks at her mother's reflection in the mirror and sees her expression of disappointment. She turns to hug her.

"Oh, I know you spent hours fixing this dress for me. But it makes me look like a child. People are going to come up and pat me on the head and say, 'Oh, what a sweet little girl,' " Shirley says, putting on a sugary, high-pitched voice. "I hate it when they do that."

Dorothy returns the hug, sighs, and strokes her daughter's hair. "All right, darling, I won't force you to wear it. It's just that you look so pretty in it."

Shirley knows her mother has given in. Her face instantly brightens. "So can I wear my jeans?"

"As long as you put on your new ones, and as long as they haven't got grass stains all over them. Then come and help us get everything ready for the guests."

"How many people are coming?"

"Oh, about a dozen, I suppose—the Honiballs, the Watsons, some of the other neighbors. The rugby starts at four p.m., so we'll start the barbecue when it's finished, at about six."

Shirley pulls a face as she changes into her jeans. "Rugby again. It's so boring, why do Dad and Charles watch it all the time? Those huge men crashing into each other and trampling on each other with their boots."

"Well, apparently the match today is very important, South Africa against New Zealand. The first big game of the season. Your father and brother are quite worked up about it. You'd think the fate of the world was in the balance." Dorothy looks at her watch. "People will start arriving soon—won't you go and unlock the gate?"

Shirley walks down the corridor, past the closed door of her brother Charles's bedroom, a guest bedroom, and a bathroom, then into the main lounge, where Charles is sitting on the couch with his back to her, watching the pregame buildup to the rugby match. Shirley ignores Charles and continues through to the kitchen, where the family's Zulu domestic servant, Salome, is peeling potatoes for the barbecue. Her broad hips sway slightly with the motion, making her long green dress swish around her ankles. The cracked skin of her bare feet is just visible below the hem. Shirley understands exactly why Salome never wears shoes— it's so much cooler and more comfortable. Dorothy always gives Salome her worn-out shoes, but the Zulu woman never puts them on.

"I'm just going to open the gate, Salome, then I'll come and help you with that."

"Thank you, little one, it's nearly finished." Salome smiles, crinkling the lines of her creased face.

Shirley doesn't mind when Salome calls her "little one," as if she were still six years old. She would forgive Salome anything; the big, slow Zulu woman has worked for the family for as long as anyone can remember, and she cared for her when she was a baby. She must be at least sixty now, Shirley thinks. She should not have to work so hard. That's one of the things Shirley dislikes about her brother: he refuses to help around the house. Never washes a dish, refuses even to make his own bed. Just expects Salome or his mother to clean up after him.

Outside, Shirley lifts her face to the balmy June sun of the southern hemisphere winter. It has not rained for a month, but the elaborate irrigation system keeps the lawns around the house green. She takes deep breaths of the cool, clean air, spiked with the tang of manure drifting on the wind from the cattle sheds, as she walks up the driveway to the entrance gate that bars access to the farmhouse. Ten feet wide and seven feet high, it has heavy gauge chain-link wire mesh stretched over a steel frame and swings from a girder the size of a section of railway track set in concrete in the ground. A coil of razor wire stretches along the top of the gate, to deter anyone trying to climb over.

The gate is part of a fence of similar strength and scale that runs in a cordon all around the farmhouse. The fence is electrified, and every thirty yards a bright yellow sign emblazoned with a grinning black skull and crossbones warns in English and Zulu that anyone touching the live wires is likely to be killed.

The gate is always kept locked, but Shirley removes the padlock now and swings the gate open so that their visitors can drive straight in. She turns and heads back indoors but has gone only ten paces when she hears drumming on the hard ground behind her, as if a buffalo were about to charge into her back.

She throws herself to the left, but the mass of hard bone and muscle under a coarse hairy coat still brushes past her ribs with enough force to push her off balance.

"Dingaan!" Shirley yells angrily at the Doberman, who has whirled to a stop in front of her and faces her now with his cropped ears erect, grinning with delight at the game. "Don't do that!"

The dog has a tennis ball in his mouth, which he drops at Shirley's feet, begging her to throw it for him. But she clicks her tongue impatiently, grabs his collar, and leads him to a wire enclosure. "Time to lock you up, or you'll try to kill all our guests."

THE DOG'S FRANTIC BARKING erupts periodically through the early afternoon as farmers from the district arrive for the barbecue in Land Rovers, Mercedes, BMWs, and four-wheel-drive pickup trucks. Dingaan hurls himself against the fence of his enclosure as each new vehicle drives past, the knob of his tail erect and vibrating with anger, his teeth exposed in gleaming white menace, foaming saliva overflowing his lips.

Shirley's father, Henry Montgomery, a stocky man who seems to be as broad as he is tall, bellows greetings to the guests and offers them beer or brandy and Coke. Some of the wives ask for white wine.

Henry ushers the men into the lounge, where chairs and sofas have been pulled up in front of the television. He is shorter than all of the guests but louder than most as he exhorts them to eat, drink, and drink some more. The women head for the kitchen, where Dorothy and Shirley are marinating lamb chops and steak for the barbecue. The noise level in the kitchen rises with each new arrival as the women shout greetings, share news from outlying farms, and compliment one another on their outfits. They ignore Salome as she stands at the sink, washing dishes by hand, an island of silence in the growing hubbub. She makes no eye contact with anyone—she knows this is not her party, and these are not her friends.

"Why don't you go and play in the garden, Shirley?" Dorothy says. "I'm sure you'd rather be outside on a lovely day like this."

Shirley pulls a sour face but does as her mother says. She has little in common with the children outside. And she knows her mother wants her to leave so the women can talk without her hearing what they say. It always strikes her as odd that her mother's friends don't want their children to know their secrets but speak loudly and freely in front of Salome, even though she is a complete stranger to most of them.

Dragging her feet, Shirley goes out into the garden to join the three children. Two boys, the Honiball brothers, age eleven and thirteen, are rolling around on the lawn, locked in combat, apparently trying to strangle each other. Shirley rolls her eyes and ignores them.

Angela Watson sits primly on a garden bench, reading a book. Her long black ringlets are tied in bows, her short white socks are topped with a frilly ruff, and her flouncy party frock reminds Shirley of the one she has just refused to put on. Shirley has never liked her; she is pompous, arrogant, spoiled. But

Shirley knows she should make an effort at being polite.

"Hi, Angela." Shirley sits next to her on the bench.

"Hello, Shirley." Angela barely looks up from her book.

"What're you reading?"

Angela doesn't bother to speak but flashes the cover of the book at Shirley.

"*Housekeeping Hints for Young Ladies*," Shirley reads out loud. "Why on earth are you reading that?"

Angela lowers the book impatiently and says in her haughtiest voice: "When you're my age, you'll realize there's more to life than just playing with dolls."

"Well, you're only one year older than me, and anyway I don't play with dolls. But even if you are so much more grown up, that's still no reason to read something so boring."

The Honiball brothers have ended their wrestling match and are now running in circles around the garden, throwing clods of dirt at each other.

"I'm preparing for the day when I get married. I'll be finished high school in four and a half years, you know."

"So you're going to finish school and immediately get married?"

"Well, not straight away, perhaps. But you never know when Mr. Right is going to come along and sweep you off your feet. And I want to be ready. You can't just start running a home without any preparation."

"But don't you want to do something more interesting than just get married and be a housewife?"

Angela does not deign to reply. She sniffs and turns the page.

Shirley sits in silence. Angela and the Honiball boys irritate her. They have come here this afternoon only because their parents were invited to the barbecue and didn't want to leave their children alone at home.

"Ah!" Shirley jerks upright with a sharp intake of breath. "Look! A *Narina trogon!*" She points excitedly toward a thorn tree thirty yards from the bench.

Angela looks up irritably and peers at the tree. "It's just a bird." She returns to her reading.

"Look at those colors!" Shirley is talking to herself. "You hardly ever see a *Narina trogon* around here." She is still admiring the rare dove-size bird when a stone whistles past it, scattering leaves and causing the bird to take off in fright.

Shirley turns and sees the elder Honiball boy lowering a catapult. "You creep!" she yells at him. "How dare you come to *my* house and try to kill *my* birds! You put that catapult away right now, or I'll shove it down your throat!"

The boy is about the same height as Shirley, but as she bears down on him, her fists clenched in anger, he quickly turns and heads for the house and the safety of the men watching rugby.

Shirley stalks off down the path that leads out of the garden and away from Angela and the Honiballs and into the thorn forest, where she can be alone with the birds and small scurrying animals of the bush.

ROBERT RUDOLPH IS THE LAST of the farmers to arrive at the Montgomery farmhouse, pulling up in his aging yellow Mercedes minutes before the rugby match is due to kick off.

"Come on, Bob," Henry shouts from the doorway as his neighbor climbs out of the car. "Why are you so late? You only live next door."

"Last-minute problem with one of the cows giving birth. They always pick the wrong moment."

Henry thrusts a can of beer into Robert's hand, slaps him on the back, and guides him through the entrance hall into the lounge. All the seats are taken, so Robert perches on the arm of a sofa. The television is turned up loud, and everyone is shouting to make themselves heard. The camera pans across the faces of the New Zealand team, standing in line at the start of the match. They look grim. Some of them mouth the words as their national anthem is played.

The crowd in Johannesburg is roaring, and Henry Montgomery's friends are roaring in his lounge. Robert tenses up as he always does at the start of a rugby game. This is the best moment of the match for him, the moment when the whole eighty minutes lie ahead, when anything is possible, when South Africa has not yet put a foot wrong. At this moment, he can still believe that this is going to be a great match, a historic match, a match in which the South Africans magically coalesce into a smooth machine that trounces the opposition. Any one of the players, or all of them, could be heroes. Maybe none of them will fumble the ball, maybe none of them will miss a tackle, maybe one of them will run seventy yards to score a spectacular try.

The New Zealand anthem ends, and the band on the pitch in Johannesburg strikes up "Nkosi Sikelel' iAfrika," the new South African anthem introduced in 1994 as an emblem of the country's transformation from apartheid to a multiracial democracy.

Robert knows the words in Zulu and begins singing along with the rugby team in Johannesburg.

The man sitting next to him on the couch, a tractor

salesman whom Robert barely knows, digs him hard in the side with his elbow. "No Mandela songs here, man!"

Robert is the only man in the room singing the anthem; the others jeer and whistle. "Turn off the volume, Henry," someone shouts. Henry lowers the volume with the remote control but does not turn it off. Robert sings the anthem to the end, refusing to be intimidated by the insults hurled at him. "Only a kaffir lover would know the words to this rubbish," declares the tractor salesman. The men in the room are boisterous, their adrenaline pumping because of the excitement of the match, their inhibitions lowered by alcohol. The tone of the comments about the anthem is generally good-natured, but the atmosphere has an edge that Robert doesn't like.

SOUTH AFRICA WINS the match, and the men leave the lounge slapping one another on the back and exchanging high-fives, united in support for their team. They walk out through the French doors and onto the patio where the barbecue has been set up, some of them staggering slightly from the effect of the brandy and beer. They regale their wives with accounts of the game; shrieks of delight and peals of laughter erupt from the house, carry to the surrounding bush, and echo briefly against the trees before being absorbed into the sounds of the African night.

The moon is rising, and Henry throws a switch to turn on the security lights. The powerful halogen lamps on twenty-foot poles throw a blaze of light around the farmhouse, turning night into day for a distance of fifty yards, illuminating the silver strands of the fence at the far end of the lawn.

Henry joins the crowd around the fire, where Robert is talking with Denis and Mary Watson, Angela's parents.

"I like your security system, Henry," Denis says. "No one'll break in here in a hurry."

"You can't be too careful," replies Henry, helping himself to grilled sausage. "I've also got a radio inside tuned to the emergency frequency, and of course I always keep my gun loaded and close at hand. Charles is a pretty good shot, too."

"You heard about the Meyers?" Denis asks. "They broke in there about ten days ago, four blacks, shot him dead, raped the wife, then killed her, too. They stole nothing but the TV and the VCR. Fortunately the kids were away at boarding school, but now they're orphans."

"What's this country coming to?" says Henry, shaking his head. "We give Mandela the country, and now his people want to murder us all."

"Come on, Henry," says Robert, "it's not that bad. Sure there's a lot of crime, but the new government has made tons of progress, especially for the poor."

"Progress?" says Denis. "Progress? I don't see any progress. The schools are getting worse, the government hospitals are a joke, our taxes just disappear into a black hole, the police are helpless to stop crime—"

"Well, the cause of the crime problem is poverty. We've got to address that first, we've got to help these masses of people who have nothing."

"Agh, it's no use trying to help them," says Henry. "Like Denis says, it's like pouring money down a bottomless pit. They don't want to help themselves, they just want to take, take, take. They think we whites owe them a living."

Robert shakes his head and takes a mouthful of curried beans. He's had this argument countless times.

"The schools are a real worry," Henry says. "Our youngest, Shirley, is in a class half full of blacks now. They've taken black kids who can barely write their own names and put them in her school, so the white kids of course are being held back. How can you study science or math if you can't add two plus two?"

"We're sending Angela to a private boarding school next year in February," interjects Mary Watson. "It's expensive, but it's the only way she's going to get a decent education. It's just awful what's going on in the government schools now, with the blacks all mixed in with the whites."

"Boarding school?" asks Henry. "Which one?"

"St. Mary's Convent in Johannesburg. It's also racially mixed, of course, but only the rich blacks can afford it, so you get a better type of black child there. At least they're properly dressed, you know, and clean."

"How much is it?"

"Twenty thousand rand a year."

Henry gives a low whistle. "That is a lot."

"I think it's worth it," Denis says. "It's the kid's future we're talking about."

"Dorothy!" Henry yells across to his wife, standing with a group of friends on the other side of the fire. "Come over here—there's something I want you to hear."

THE NEXT MORNING at breakfast, Henry has a headache and a thirst that refuses to be quenched. "Where's Charles?" he asks gruffly.

"Still in bed. You shouldn't have let him drink so much beer last night, Henry."

He grunts. "He's old enough to look after himself. It's good for him to suffer the consequences of his actions. If he drinks too much, he'll get a hangover. It's a basic lesson."

"But he's not even seventeen yet."

"You spoil that boy, Dorothy. You can't protect him all his life. He needs to stand on his own two feet, and you're never too young to do that."

Dorothy pours more coffee for her husband and tries to steer the conversation elsewhere. "Did you enjoy the barbecue, Shirley?"

"The food was great. Pity about the company."

"What do you mean, dear?"

"Those Honiball boys are so childish, I hate them. They were shooting at birds with their catapults. And Angela Watson is stuck up and boring."

Her father breaks in, clearing his throat loudly. "That reminds me, Shirley. Your mother and I were talking last night, and we've decided you should go to boarding school next year."

Shirley drops her fork, spilling scrambled egg. Her eyes widen in horror, her mouth opens in protest but nothing comes out. For a minute, no one at the table speaks.

"What?" It sounds like a croak. "What do you mean, Dad, boarding school?"

"It might be difficult at first, dear, but—"

"Boarding school." Henry interrupts his wife. "It means boarding school, just that. We've decided to send you to one because the local schools are hopeless, as you know. Full of ignorant black kids bringing standards down."

"But . . . but . . . I *can't*, Dad." Shirley's breaking voice shows she is on the verge of tears. "This is my home here, I'm happy here, why . . . why . . ."

"We've decided, Shirley, and that's that. You'd better just get used to the idea. You're going when the next school year starts in February. St. Mary's in Johannesburg, where the Watson girl is going."

Shirley's face crumples in misery, and wood screeches against wood as she pushes her chair away from the table and runs from the room, tears pouring down her cheeks.

Henry scowls at his plate but goes on eating. "She can cry all she wants, but my mind's made up. It's for her own good."

"Really, we could have broken it to her more gently, Henry."

Dorothy gives her husband a cross look as she gets up from her chair and goes after Shirley. She finds her daughter lying facedown on her bed, sobbing into her pillow.

"Shirley dear, Shirley, listen to me."

"You hate me!" The words are muffled by the pillow. "You're sending me away because you hate me."

"Oh no, Shirley, don't say that, you know that's not true." Dorothy massages her daughter's back, trying to rub her love into the tight muscles.

"But then why do I have to go to boarding school? I don't want to go away!"

"It's only because we think it's best for you, Shirley. You know how standards have fallen at the schools around here—"

"I don't care! I don't care! I just want to stay here, with you, Mommy, and Salome, and—and with Dad, of course, and the bush. How can I go and live in some horrible dormitory in Johannesburg, so far from here?" Shirley moans into her pillow with new despair, sobs shaking her body. "It'll be like going to jail."

Dorothy doesn't know what to say. "You'll be able to come home for the holidays."

Shirley will not be consoled. "You hate me, you hate me, you hate me," she sobs.

Dorothy sighs. "One day, one day you'll be grateful. When you're a doctor, or a company executive, when you're making a good living, when you're independent, truly free, then you'll be grateful that you went to a good school."

Shirley hears something in her mother's voice that she has never heard before, a kind of longing, a wistful note of regret, that stills her crying.

ALTER NGUGU REVS THE ENGINE of his To-
yota taxi van impatiently, drowning the
dawn chorus of doves and crickets and
spewing clouds of diesel exhaust into the
fresh morning breeze. He can feel winter is over, that
today will be hot. Maybe the rain will come this afternoon, a thunderstorm to break the drought. July and
August were the driest months he can remember. They
are halfway into September now, with only a few light
showers so far, hardly enough to dampen the dust
around the huts.

Walter slams the heel of his hand on the horn, and
at last Lindiwe, Tendeka, Mandisa, and Vusi come run-

ning out of the kraal toward the van. "Come, children, come quickly!" he shouts as they run up, school bags swinging from their shoulders.

He has to be in Tugela Ferry, the main village of the Msinga district, in thirty minutes to pick up his first load of passengers, and to get there on time, he should have left five minutes ago. Now he is going to have to drive like a maniac on the rutted, potholed gravel road, because the children are late. Petrus is already in the taxi. He has just finished school and is going into the city with his father to look for work on a construction site. He is also impatient, because jobs are few and you get one only if you are among the first in line at the employment office.

The girls clamber into the van, but Vusi holds back.

"Father, I think I'll walk to school."

"What? Walk three miles? Have you gone crazy?"

"I get sick in the van, Father. I think it's the bumping on the rough road. I would prefer to walk. Really, it's not so far."

"Suit yourself."

Walter shakes his head to show he cannot understand why his son is being so foolish. But he is late and has no time to argue. If the boy wants to walk, let him walk. He puts the van in gear and pulls off in a cloud of dust.

"What's this about Vusi getting sick?" he shouts over his shoulder to the girls in the back. "He's never said anything about it before."

The girls giggle behind their hands, digging their elbows into one another's ribs.

"What?" demands Walter. "What's the joke? What's going on?"

"It's a secret," Mandisa shrieks. "We can't tell you." The girls collapse in giggles again.

"Tell me now what's going on, now, or Petrus will throw you all out of the door and you can all walk."

Petrus half rises from his seat as if to carry out the threat.

"Promise you won't tell Mother?" asks Lindiwe.

"Just tell me."

"Vusi has a dog!" The three girls yell it out in one voice. "He keeps it as a pet and feeds it and plays with it all day," says Lindiwe. "But please don't tell Mother. If she knew, she would take a stick and beat Vusi. And she would chase the dog away."

Walter chuckles to himself.

"A dog?" he asks over his shoulder. "What kind of dog?"

"Just a dog," says Tendeka.

"Vusi says it's a very special dog," Lindiwe interjects. "He says it's going to be the best hunting dog in

Msinga. He says it's the cleverest dog he's ever seen."

"He's been hiding it in the bush, keeping it in a hole when he's at school," Mandisa explains. "But now the dog's too big to stay in a hole all morning, so he wants to take it to school with him. That's why he wants to walk."

"Where did he get this dog?" Walter asks.

"It was one of Sheba's puppies, one that the leopard didn't eat," Lindiwe replies.

"What? One of Sheba's puppies?" Walter slows the taxi and looks at Lindiwe in the rearview mirror. "It can't be—the leopard killed them all."

"No, Vusi found one right at the bottom of the hole. But it only has three legs."

"Three legs? Why three legs?"

"The leopard hurt it but didn't kill it. Vusi and Granny helped to heal it, but they had to cut off his foot. The right-hand one, at the back."

Walter digests the information. His first reaction is anger at his son for keeping the puppy's existence hidden from him.

"Why didn't he tell me about this puppy?"

"We told you," Tendeka says. "Because Mommy would kill it if she knew. He couldn't tell anyone, except us."

Walter had been sorry to lose Sheba—and the

money Shakes would have paid him. Perhaps he could sell Shakes this puppy of Vusi's? He considers the idea only briefly before rejecting it. Shakes wouldn't want a dog with three legs. No one would. Vusi should have just put the puppy in a sack with a heavy stone and thrown it into the river. How could a crippled dog ever be of any use?

They are at the school now, and Walter stops to drop off the girls. He is smiling. Maybe a three-legged dog is useless, but at least Vusi is showing the right Zulu instincts. Keeping the dog shows that he must be keen to start hunting.

Walter turns to Petrus. "How old is Vusi now?"

"Nearly twelve."

"He's getting big. Soon he'll be ready to go hunting with us. But he'll have to get a new dog somewhere."

Vusi is breathing heavily by the time he arrives at the school. He has had to jog most of the way to get there on time. Gillette is at his side, panting but eager to explore the smells of this new world. Vusi's plan is to find a patch of shade within sight of the school building, then tell the dog to lie down and stay there while he attends class. With any luck, no one will even notice he has brought his dog to school.

"Vusi Ngugu! Come here, boy!"

Vusi's heart sinks as the voice of one of the two teachers, Agnes Sithole, rings across the playground.

"Stay," he whispers to Gillette, then trots across to the teacher.

Agnes is a big woman who dresses in long, brightly colored caftans that sweep the ground and rustle loudly as she strides around the school. She wears a turbanlike headdress that makes her look even taller than she is.

"Good morning, Mrs. Sithole." Vusi stares at the ground, too nervous to meet the teacher's glare.

"What is that dog doing there?"

Vusi puts on the most innocent, angelic look he can muster. He turns and looks across at the spot where Gillette is lying, as though he's not sure what dog she's talking about.

"Oh, that dog. That's my dog," Vusi says, feigning surprise. "He must have followed me from home. But he'll be all right there, Mrs. Sithole, he won't bother anyone."

Agnes Sithole draws a deep breath as if she is gathering her strength for a tirade and lifts her arm to point at the dog.

"I will not have—"

She stops in midsentence, her face suddenly transforming from anger to disgust. Gillette is on his feet, still on the spot where Vusi told him to stay, but straining forward like a spring under tension. His ears are up, his nose is pointing, his tail is straight out behind him, and his whole body is quivering with excitement.

Vusi is puzzled—Gillette has never done this before. Then he sees what both Gillette and his teacher are staring at. A fat gray rat is scuttling away from the classrooms, crossing the playground toward the bush surrounding the school. Half a dozen children catch sight of it and scream. The children often see rats at the school. Their holes are everywhere; they are attracted to the school by the crumbs left over from the children's lunches. The teachers put traps out for them, but the rodents seem to know they are dangerous and seldom get caught. One boy throws a stone at the retreating rat but misses by several feet.

Without thinking, Vusi yells at Gillette: "Geddit!"

The dog breaks from the spot like a hundred-meter sprinter out of the starting blocks, scrabbling for traction with its three feet. Vusi groans. Gillette is running as fast as he can, but he is moving far too slowly to catch his prey. The rat scuttles closer to the treeline, a yard or less from safety. Gillette sees that the rat is getting away. Straining to extract every last ounce of strength from his body, he gathers himself up and launches himself into the air. The six-foot leap closes the gap, and both of Gillette's front feet come down on the fleeing rat, snapping its back. Gillette snatches the rodent up in his jaws and shakes it once to break its neck and make sure it is dead. He drops the lifeless rat onto the ground and looks up at Vusi, eyes shining, as if to say: "How about that?"

"Good boy!" Vusi shouts. "Good boy!"

Vusi can barely contain the pride that is bursting within him. Gillette, at nine months, is no longer a puppy. This morning he has shown he is a dog, a real dog, and that he can overcome the handicap of his missing leg. Vusi turns to the teacher.

"You see, Mrs. Sithole? Do you see how good he is? He will help keep the school free of rats."

She does not reply immediately, but she is smiling slightly when she claps her hands and announces loudly, "Come, come, children, we are late. Everybody inside, it's time to begin."

Then to Vusi she says: "Your dog killed that rat, so you are the one who must throw it away."

Vusi runs off to collect the rat and throw it deep into the bush for some scavenging animal to find and devour. His heart is light—Mrs. Sithole did not say Gillette could stay at the school, but neither did she order him to take the dog away. Vusi knows that that is her way of giving permission.

THE SCHOOL CONSISTS of just two classrooms, one for each teacher. After he has thrown away the rat, Vusi rushes into Agnes's class. Because he is the last one in, there are no empty desks, and he has to join some of the other children who are sitting on the floor, their books out in front of them. About forty children, ranging in age from six to twelve, are crammed into the room. Several windows are broken, and when it rains, the roof leaks in two places.

Agnes has already started the class when Vusi comes in. He sinks down on a spot near the open door, so he can sneak glances at Gillette, who is back in his stay position under a shade tree.

"Somebody tell Vusi the rat-catcher what he has missed." The class titters at the label their teacher has given Vusi. One boy sitting in back raises his hand.

"Yes, Richard?"

"We were learning about Bambata, madam."

"Yes, and who was he?"

"He was a great Zulu chief, like Shaka. He was always fighting."

"He led a rebellion, yes. Against whom was the rebellion?"

"The whites."

"The British, Richard, the British. They came to Zululand two hundred years ago, by sea, and landed on the coast. Slowly they moved inland, farther and farther. As they moved, they took the land from the Zulus. They pushed the Zulus into a smaller and smaller area."

The teacher pauses, gazing around the room to see that everyone is paying attention.

"Vusi, what do you think happened next?"

The boy gives a startled gasp. He had been craning his head around to see what Gillette was doing.

"Um, I don't know, Mrs. Sithole."

"What was I talking about?"

Vusi hesitates. "Chief . . . Bambam?"

"Bambata! Bambata! He was one of the greatest Zulus, and you can't even remember his name! You must look at me, not at that dog! If you look out the door once more, you will go straight home, and take that dog with you, and that dog will never be allowed near here again. Do you understand?"

"Yes, Mrs. Sithole. Sorry, Mrs. Sithole."

"So. To return to the lesson. One hundred years ago the British started making us, the Zulus, pay taxes to them. No one could afford these taxes. There was much dissatisfaction. So in 1906 Bambata led a rebellion against the British."

She pauses again and repeats: "Vusi, what do you think happened then?"

He is ready this time. "Bambata must have lost the rebellion, because the Zulus are still poor, we still pay taxes, and we do not have enough land." Vusi has often heard his father complain about land and taxes.

"Yes, we still pay taxes, but now we pay them to a government that we voted for, so that's all right. We have to pay taxes so the government has money for hospitals, roads, salaries, and schools."

Agnes looks around the classroom with its peeling paint, missing panes, and dilapidated desks and frowns. Not much government spending has reached Msinga, she thinks. The education budget is all spent in the cities, where the children of the government officials go to school. The people in the countryside have to make do with what's left over, if anything.

"You are right, Bambata lost the rebellion. His men were armed with sticks, ox-hide shields, and spears. The British troops had guns—it was no contest. That is why we live as we do today, the Zulus all pushed onto small parcels of land, while the whites who are descended from the British settlers have big farms."

Vusi ponders this. "But ma'am, my father says that we won our country back in 1994, when we voted for President Mandela. He says we are not ruled by the whites anymore, that they cannot order us around like they used to when there was apartheid."

"That's true, South Africa is a democracy now. We have majority rule. But the question of who owns the land has not been settled. If you take something by force, do you have the right to claim it as your own? Do you have the right to say later, as the white farmers do, 'Yes, you can have the land back, but you must pay for it'? When we blacks are too poor?" Agnes's voice is growing heated. "It's taking us a long time to fix all the problems created by the white conquest of our country all those hundreds of years ago, and by apartheid."

WALTER NGUGU DRIVES through the outskirts of Tugela Ferry, a hamlet of perhaps a hundred shacks, a dozen shops, a post office, and a police station strung out along one of the few paved highways through this part of Zululand. Many years ago it was a thriving trading post that owed its importance to the river ferry, which at the time was one of the few means for travelers to cross the Tugela. Now the ferry is long gone, there are plenty of bridges across the river, and the hamlet has retreated back into obscurity.

Walter stops his van at the taxi rank, and the waiting crowd jostles to climb in. The van is licensed to carry fourteen passengers, but Walter lets eighteen people onboard before he closes the door and pulls off on the ninety-minute ride to Pietermaritzburg, the nearest big city. The more people he can squeeze in, the more money he makes in fares.

He knows most of his passengers. They ride into the city every day to their jobs, because there is no work in Tugela Ferry or its surroundings, where the only honest living to be made is from subsistence farming with vegetables and goats. Deep in the remote valleys and high on the inaccessible mountainsides, some Zulus grow marijuana—known locally as *dagga*—which they sell in Pietermaritzburg or farther afield in Durban or Johannesburg. Sometimes police aircraft fly over the plantations spraying herbicide, but generally they leave this lawless area to itself.

There is lots of money in marijuana, but Walter is not interested. The trade is run by hard men, criminals who think nothing of eliminating their competitors. To eliminate, in this part of the world, means to kill.

"So how are things today, *madala*?" Walter asks over his shoulder to the man in the seat behind him, Shadrack Buthelezi, as the taxi enters the open country outside Tugela Ferry.

"We are suffering, brother, we are suffering." Buthelezi's lined face is propped on the walking stick he holds between his knees. "Every day the price of food goes up, but my wages stay the same. On the radio I hear talk about recession and inflation. What are these things, brother, recession and inflation? They are killing me."

"Oh, I know, I know. Look at the price of gasoline. It is sky-high now, sky-high. This trip, for example. After I have paid for the gasoline, maybe I'll have a profit of thirty or forty rand from fares. Forty rand for a ninety-minute journey. That is nothing, nothing. We are working like slaves." Walter shakes his head in despair.

"You know what I'm thinking." Buthelezi leans forward and lowers his voice. "I'm thinking I might take some *dagga* into Pietermaritzburg to sell. That's the only way to beat this recession monster."

"No, *madala*, no, don't do that. If you get caught, you go to jail. If you don't get caught, you get into trouble anyway. The people involved with that are very evil, they are greedy." Walter pauses to shift gears, and the engine tone changes as the Toyota strains up the start of a long, curving hill. He continues, "Greed makes people rotten, *madala*. I know, because it is happening with the taxis. Up to now we taxi drivers in Tugela Ferry have worked together well. We don't steal passengers from each other. We know each other, we trust each other. We are almost like a family."

The taxi has no air conditioning, and the early summer heat is building inside the crowded van. Walter rolls down his window to let in the breeze.

"But now strangers are coming in. Maybe you have seen them. They come from Pietermaritzburg and try to take our passengers. It's not good, *madala*. There are not enough passengers for the taxi drivers already in Tugela Ferry. If more taxis come from Pietermaritzburg, then we will really starve. All because some people are too greedy."

Walter shakes his head. "It's getting worse. The Pietermaritzburg drivers are threatening us. They say we must find other routes to work, and if we don't . . ." Walter extends his index finger in imitation of a gun and points it at his own head.

The taxi is passing through the outlying suburbs of the city now. A traffic officer steps into the road ahead and signals the vehicle to pull over. Walter curses under his breath as he complies.

The officer walks slowly around the taxi, looking carefully through the dust-caked windows. He comes back to stand beside the driver's door.

"You have a lot of passengers today."

"Yes, quite a few. I did not count them."

"I can see eighteen. That's four too many."

Walter just sighs and doesn't bother to reply.

"You know I should give you a big fine. I should write out a ticket, fifty rand for every passenger over the limit. That's two hundred rand."

Walter gives the officer a tired smile. He has been through this procedure many times before. "Don't go to all the trouble of writing a ticket, officer. Let me just give you cash now." He hands the policeman a twenty-rand note. "Okay?"

The traffic officer folds the note and tucks it into his pocket. "Drive safely," he says, smirking.

ON HIS SECOND RETURN TRIP of the day from Pietermaritzburg, Walter has only eight passengers, barely enough to pay for gasoline. The bribe he had to pay the traffic officer means he will probably not make any money today at all. Petrus could not find a job. He trudged around the city for hours, but everywhere the story was the same: no work.

Walter is in a foul mood, roughly slamming the van into high gear for the long, straight downhill stretch into Tugela Ferry. He barely notices the car in his rearview mirror until it starts to overtake him at high speed.

"Fool!" he shouts across at the car, though he knows the driver cannot hear him. It is a BMW, not a recent model but much faster than his taxi. The car stays level with the taxi. Walter looks again to see what the driver is playing at.

He cannot see through the tinted windows of the black BMW, but then the passenger-side window is lowered, and a gun muzzle is thrust out.

The passengers in the taxi see the gun and scream. Walter slams on his brakes, and the van swerves off the road. Miraculously it remains upright as it comes to a stop, the front fender resting against a tree. Walter and the passengers tumble out the door, in shock but unharmed.

The passengers hold on to each other for support, their hearts beating wildly, their breath coming in deep gulps. They raise their voices, talking rapidly and loudly as if this will purge their stress. The babble subsides and coalesces into one question: Who were those people? Who were they?

Walter stands alone, bowed, silently contemplating his damaged Toyota and the flat tire, already wondering where he can borrow money for the repairs. He knows who the men in the BMW were: rival taxi drivers from the city.

THE FOUR DOGS of the Ngugu kraal are on their feet, tails sweeping from side to side, ears lifted. Spear and Beauty make mock grabs for each other's throats, then shake their coats as if trying to release the tension building inside them. The dogs have read the signs: it's hunting time.

Two days after the taxi was forced off the road, Walter and Petrus stand outside the kitchen hut in the twilight, tapping their legs with the ends of their homemade spears. The weapons are about three feet long, smooth teak sticks tipped with sharp metal points. Walter has a long knife in his belt. Both hunters are unusually nervous, and they wear antelope-skin amulets to ensure that their dead ancestors will watch over them in the dangerous enterprise they are about to undertake.

Prudence emerges from the kitchen, carrying enamel mugs of steaming coffee for her husband and son. They take them gratefully, warming their hands against the hot mugs in the evening chill.

"Do you really have to do this, Walter?"

"What choice is there, wife? Without the van, I cannot work. To fix the van, I need eight hundred rand. Where will I get that money? Only one place."

Walter takes a gulp of coffee so he does not have to meet his wife's angry eyes.

"You say you don't want to sell *dagga* because it's a crime. Well, this is also a crime."

"Look how rich the white farmers are. Look how

many cattle they have, look how many we have. Do not forget, this was all our land once." Walter's hand sweeps across the horizon. "Then the settlers came and took it from us at gunpoint. If they can take our whole country by force, why can't I take one or two of their cows? They have so many, they won't even miss them."

"But it's dangerous, Walter. What will I do if I lose my husband and my eldest son?"

"Don't worry, Mother, we will both come back," Petrus assures her. "We will bring two fat cows, we can eat good meat again."

Walter and Petrus drain their mugs, whistle to the dogs, and set off with them into the bush. The men are barely out of sight of the kraal when they hear the sound of a small creature hurrying toward them.

Strangely, the dogs ignore the sound, as if it were something of no concern, but the men turn with their spears ready.

"It's me, Father, it's me." Vusi emerges from the trees, Gillette at his heels. "Please, Father, can I come with you? I'm old enough now to hunt. I'm twelve, and look, I have a dog."

Vusi has been nervous about this moment, knowing for months that one day he would have to reveal Gillette's existence to his father. Deciding it was better to get it over with sooner rather than later, he had screwed up his courage and brought Gillette to the path through the bush that he knew his father and brother would take.

Walter laughs. "So this is your dog."

"He's called Gillette, Father, because his teeth are so sharp. I've been training him, and he's ready to hunt."

"Where did you find this dog?"

This is the question Vusi has been dreading. He swallows hard.

"He is one of Sheba's puppies. When the leopard killed her, he left Gillette. But now he is missing part of his leg. I—I couldn't tell anyone about him, Father, because I didn't want to lose him. Mother wanted me to kill him, but I couldn't."

Walter steps closer to the dog and studies him.

"Yes, it is definitely a Sheba dog. You can see that. What a pity about the leg. It will never be any good for hunting."

"He will, Father, he will! We'll show you tonight!"

"No, Vusi, you are not old enough, especially for this hunt. We are going somewhere dangerous tonight. Soon you will start hunting, be patient. But that dog . . ." Walter shakes his head without finishing the sentence. He and Petrus walk on, leaving Vusi behind. Gillette, sensing the boy's disappointment, lifts his head and licks his hand.

AN HOUR LATER Walter and Petrus come to a barbed-wire fence separating the bush from cattle pasture. Walter uses wire cutters to sever all six strands, and the men and dogs cross onto the white farmer's land. The plan is to find the cattle herd, separate two beasts from it, and herd them back through the opening in the fence. They know the farm belongs to a man called Rudolph, and they have chosen it because it is close, but also because the owner has a reputation around the district for being slow to lose his temper. They hope that by raiding this farm, their chances of being shot by an armed, angry farmer will be reduced.

Walter and Petrus head toward the lights of the main farm buildings. As they get closer, they hear the cattle shifting in pens where they have been herded for the night. The men move warily, because the farmers of the district invariably post a night watchman, a Zulu like themselves, to guard the livestock and the homestead.

They pause ten yards from the wire fence of the cattle pen, all senses alert. They hear voices from the homestead on the far side of the pen. The watchman must be talking to the farmer, Walter thinks. Watchman and farmer will have their attention focused on each other, and they might not hear unusual sounds from the cattle pen. There is no better time to strike than now.

Walter silently cuts through the wire—only four strands here. The cattle closest to them are uneasy, lowing in alarm as they smell the dogs. Walter had considered coming without dogs, but he calculated they would be valuable on the way home to help keep the stolen beasts moving quickly.

He orders the dogs to wait, then dashes into the pen with Petrus. They throw ropes around the necks of the two closest cows. Petrus pulls the animals toward the gap in the pen while his father pokes them from behind with his spear. The cattle in the pen are lowing and milling about in confusion. Walter hears a door slam in the distance. They do not have much to fear from the Zulu watchman—he will be armed only with a stick. But the farmer will have a gun.

The two cows they have roped are obstinate, refusing to leave the herd. Precious seconds are lost fighting the animals, until finally the cows break from the pen, eyes rolling wildly. Their instinct is to stampede, and

Petrus is pulled off his feet. One of the cows breaks free of his grasp and gallops off into the dark.

"Leave it," Walter tells his son. "Let's go now, fast."

The two men both grab the rope attached to the remaining cow and start off into the night, the dogs snapping at the cow's heels.

"Halt! Halt!" The cries ring out in Zulu from the farmhouse.

Walter and Petrus keep running, the cow bellowing as it lumbers after them.

The farmer is shooting now. Walter counts three shots, but the farmer cannot see them, and he is too far away to be able to aim.

The final shot is followed by a soft thud from the darkness behind them and a high-pitched howl of surprise and pain from one of the dogs. The men keep running with their prize.

Once through the fence and in the protection of the bush, they stop and listen for sounds of pursuit. Nothing. Walter checks the dogs. Charcoal is missing. He gives a low whistle, in case she is nearby, but there is no response.

"That was a good dog," Petrus says. "Not so fast but very brave, very strong."

His father grunts in agreement. "Let's wait five minutes. Maybe she's still coming."

They wait ten minutes, then move on. They have lost a dog but gained a cow. By the time it has been slaughtered and the meat and hide sold in Tugela Ferry, Walter should have enough money to get his taxi back on the road.

CHAPTER

4

VUSI SHIVERS IN FEAR when his father tells the family about the hunt the next morning over breakfast. "The farmer shot at least ten times!" Walter says. Petrus struggles to keep himself from smiling and looks down at his plate so no one will see his mirth. The hunt was truly frightening, but his father always likes to embellish events so they sound even more dramatic than they really were. "We counted the bullets, didn't we, Petrus?" Walter looks over at his eldest son for confirmation. Petrus nods rapidly in agreement, his face averted still. "Some of the bullets were so close, they kicked up the sand at our feet," Walter adds.

Vusi is wide-eyed at the tale and the risks his father and brother had run. If you came upon a leopard while you were hunting, you at least had a chance to stab it with your spear and either kill it or drive it off. But if you came across an angry white man with a gun, what chance did you have?

For the next couple of days, Vusi thinks about little else but the danger of hunting on the neighboring white farms. Would he ever be brave enough to go with his brother and his father on a hunt like that? Would he disgrace himself by showing everyone he was a coward?

His father told the story on Wednesday morning. By Saturday Vusi knows what he has to do. He finishes breakfast quickly and hurries into the bush, whistling for Gillette. He keeps a tight grip on his *kierie*. The stick has psychological value but little else. Vusi could kill a snake with it, if necessary, but against a man with a gun, it is nothing.

After an hour's walking, Vusi and Gillette are far from the trails they usually follow. They are in unknown territory, where the bush of the Zulu reservation gives way to the fenced farms of the white game and cattle ranchers.

Vusi has decided there is only one way to overcome his fear of white farmers. He will, for the first time in his life, cross the fence onto one of their farms to prove to himself that he is not scared. He will not approach the farmhouse, go near the cattle, or let anyone see him. But he must find the courage to cross the fence.

Suddenly he is face to face with six shiny new strands of barbed wire. This must be the spot where his father and Petrus cut the fence on the night of their cattle raid. It has been repaired already. Maybe the farmer is still watching this place.

Vusi is tempted to turn around and go home, but Gillette's presence comforts him. "Okay, boy, we can do it." The dog looks up, eyes bright, tail wagging. "Be careful, Gillette. Don't be afraid. I am with you."

Vusi gives a final look around, then drops to the ground and scrambles under the fence on his belly. He pulls the two bottom strands of wire apart for Gillette to follow him through.

The boy's heart is pounding in his chest. Then it stops completely as a crow gives a startled, raucous cry in the branches above and flaps on heavy wings to a distant tree.

Vusi forces himself to breathe deeply and slowly. He closes his eyes and conjures up a mental picture of Shaka, the fearless king of the Zulus who defeated anyone who stood in his way. With the blood of such a warrior in his veins, how can he be scared?

The boy pushes out his chest and walks on, following the line of the fence. Gradually his heartbeat and breathing return to normal. This is just like walking to school. No problem.

Why should I stick to the fence? he asks himself. I am not a frightened little boy. I am a great hunter. And I have my brave dog with me. I will go a little deeper into this farm.

Vusi turns away from the fence, following a line of trees along a dry riverbed. There is no danger here, he can walk confidently and quickly. He comes to another fence.

A white man's fence? So what. I have no fear of fences. Vusi parts the wires and clambers through. He does not know it, but he has just crossed from the Rudolph farm onto the Montgomery property.

Emboldened by his own daring, Vusi pushes through the bush until he comes to a well-worn path. He picks a direction at random and smiles down at Gillette. "Exciting, hey, boy? We can face any danger, nothing scares us!"

Vusi begins whistling brightly and picks up his pace. He skips down the path, the momentum of his joy pushing him faster and faster—so fast that as he turns a bend in the path, he fails to see an exposed tree root and trips, falling flat onto the dusty ground.

"Who are you?" Vusi freezes at the voice. The next thing he will hear, he knows, is the blast of a gun, and then he will be dead. He hopes Gillette will be able to get away safely.

He tenses and waits, but nothing happens. Just that voice again, repeating the question.

It isn't a Zulu voice, and it isn't a man's voice.

Vusi, still lying on his stomach where he had fallen, slowly turns his head. Above him stands a white girl, about his size. She has striking blond hair and pale blue eyes that seem to see into his heart. Vusi thinks he can feel the energy of her eyes flutter inside him. He wonders if she is a witch.

He pushes himself up to his knees, bowing his head so he won't have to look into those eyes. Gillette is standing next to him, head cocked, waiting to see what happens next.

"You're not one of the laborers' children, are you?"

The language is unintelligible to Vusi. He has learned some English at school, but this girl speaks too fast. He thinks about turning tail and running, back across the fence. But maybe the girl's father is around, with his gun. Worse, how would that look if he, Vusi, ran away from a girl? He could never live with the shame.

He forces himself to look into her frowning face.

"Vusi," he says, pointing to himself. "Vusi."

The girl's frown slowly eases, her face lightens.

"Shirley," the girl replies, pointing to herself. "Shirley."

Vusi repeats her name, haltingly. She smiles.

"Gillette," he says, pointing to the dog. "Gillette."

"Gillette? Like a razor blade?" The girl mimes shaving.

Vusi nods enthusiastically. The girl can speak Zulu! She knows what a Gillette is!

Vusi and Shirley look at each other, smiling, but not knowing how to proceed.

"Where do you live?" Shirley asks.

Vusi lifts his shoulders in the universal signal of in-comprehension.

Shirley repeats the question more slowly, still with no success. She is determined to communicate with this boy who has stumbled into her life. Inspiration strikes: the interpreters she has seen on television who translate news programs into sign language for the deaf!

"Where?" she says, lifting her palms at shoulder height and looking around questioningly.

Vusi watches carefully. He realizes she is asking a question, a question about place, judging by the way she is looking around.

"You," Shirley says, pointing at him.

"Live," she says. "Live." How to convey *live* in sign language? Her eyes light up as she thinks of the answer.

"Live," she repeats, then puts her hands together and places them against her right cheek, which she tilts to one side. She closes her eyes and snores gently.

Vusi nods vigorously to show he understands. "Sleep," he says in Zulu. "Sleep."

Shirley puts the gestures together in sequence: "Where . . . you . . . live?"

Light dawns on Vusi's face. "Where do I sleep? Where do I sleep? Over there," he says in Zulu, pointing in the direction where he thinks the kraal lies.

But Shirley looks confused, and Vusi realizes just pointing into the bush is not an adequate explanation.

He falls to his knees and smooths out a flat area of sand in the path. Taking a stick, he draws a small circle to show where they are now. Then he adds a winding line for the path, a line going off at a tangent, then a fence, then a winding line again, another fence, and a short line that ends in a bigger circle. He smiles up at her triumphantly.

Shirley studies the drawing carefully. She works out that if he has crossed two fences, he must have come across the Rudolph farm and must live somewhere just beyond that.

Vusi points at Shirley silently, searching for the word she used five minutes ago. "You!" he shouts in English, thrilled that he has remembered it. "You! Where?" He can't recall the final word, but Shirley has already dropped to the ground beside him and is drawing a map of how to get to her house.

When Shirley gets home that day, she is torn between excitement at the encounter, the fun they had communicating across the language barrier, and trepidation at what her parents would say about a black stranger trespassing on the farm.

I'll tell Mom and Dad that the boy got lost and crossed onto the farm by mistake, which is probably the truth anyway, she thinks. If he spoke better English, he could have told me what he was doing here. Or if I spoke better Zulu. But he was so nice, he couldn't possibly have meant any harm. I'll tell Mom and Dad that, too. But they'll probably be suspicious anyway, especially Dad.

Shirley wanders into the kitchen, where Dorothy and Salome are getting ready to carry dinner to the dining room.

"Hi, Mom. Hi, Salome."

"There you are at last—you're late again. Help me carry these potatoes in, then sit down to eat."

Her mother cuts Shirley off before she can tell them about meeting Vusi.

Maybe there'll be a chance during dinner, she thinks. But her heart sinks when she hears the screen door bang shut like a gunshot. Only her father swings the door shut with such force, and only when he is in a foul mood.

He stomps heavily through the house and into the dining room, his boots squeaking sharply on the polished hardwood floors. He grunts a greeting to Shirley, grabs the chair at the head of the table with a broad hand, scrapes it back, and sits down. Charles follows him into the room and sits next to Shirley.

Shirley's mother comes in with the last of the food, thick well-cooked steaks, and puts one on each plate.

"Shirley, it's your turn to say grace," her mother says.

"For what we are about to receive, may the Lord make us truly thankful, amen."

Silence falls over the table as the family starts to eat.

"Blast!" Shirley's father shoves his plate away from him, rattling the tableware.

"What's the matter, dear?"

"This damned steak is overcooked again! When is that bloody incompetent woman going to learn how to cook a steak properly? How many years has she been working for us, and she still can't get it right!"

His wife sighs. "Salome tries her best. Perhaps she was trying to do too much and left the steaks under the grill too long. Here, take mine—it's still a bit pink inside, the way you like it." She puts her steak on his plate and takes his for herself. The atmosphere of anger still hangs over the table, but everyone resumes eating.

"Bloody kaffirs," Shirley's father mutters.

"Really, Henry, you shouldn't call them that any-more. It's not nice. And if anyone outside this room were to hear you—"

"I can still say and do what I like inside my own house, I hope."

"It's not a good example for the children."

"The children might as well know what a bunch of incompetents we employ, just like the bunch of black idiots running the country now."

"The black kids in my class are really dumb," Charles chimes in.

Shirley feels uncomfortable when her family starts talking like this. She tries to change the subject.

"Bad day on the farm, Dad?"

Henry rolls his eyes.

"What, apart from the fact that it's the end of September and the rains haven't come yet?" He takes a bite of steak. He carries on talking as he chews. "Well, Elijah was plowing the fields to put the corn in, when the tractor broke down. The John Deere, the big one. Guess what? Bloody fool hadn't checked if there was oil in the transmission. He'd been plowing all day with no oil. It's a ten-thousand-rand repair job, at least."

"More peas, anyone?" Shirley's mother interjects.

But her husband won't be diverted from his tirade. His face is reddening.

"If a black man doesn't even know how to run a tractor, no wonder they're making such a mess of running the country. Lazy, corrupt bunch of thieves and idiots. Look what a mess they've made since 1994. The hospitals don't work, the standard of schooling is appalling, there's no law and order whatsoever. They're not like us."

To Shirley's relief, the telephone rings in the next room, and her father goes to answer it. Otherwise he could have kept on for another fifteen minutes about the failings of black South Africans.

His voice is muffled by the thick walls of the farmhouse, but they hear him talking in excited tones on the telephone, his anger apparently forgotten.

Henry is beaming when he returns to the room. "That was St. Mary's," he says, looking at Shirley. "Good news—they have a place for you next year."

Shirley's heart contracts, and the food in her mouth threatens to choke her. The joy of meeting Vusi and Gillette is snuffed out in an instant. Ever since her parents first announced the boarding school plan in June, Shirley had been clinging to one hope: that St. Mary's would be full and would turn down her application. Now that last possible reprieve is gone.

"Don't look so downhearted, dear."

"Have you still not gotten used to the idea, for goodness' sake!" Henry demands, cutting in on his wife. "You don't know how lucky you are to get in at St. Mary's. Hundreds of girls would give their eyeteeth for the opportunity you're getting. And don't forget, we're paying a lot of money for you. You can show some gratitude, instead of sulking about it."

Dorothy lays a hand on Henry's arm to calm him down. Shirley stares at her plate. She counts off the months in her mind: October, November, December,

January . . . February. She knows if she tries to say anything, she will break down in tears.

THE NEXT DAY, Sunday, Shirley wakes up thinking about Vusi. She can't remember what she dreamed, but it must have been something about him and his dog. She discovers that if she holds an image of Vusi and Gillette in her mind, it almost blots out the despair about being sent away to boarding school. She thinks about the boy while she brushes her teeth—he has such an amazing white smile—and while she has her breakfast—I wonder if he also has bacon and eggs every morning?

As soon as she finishes eating, she hurries out of the house and across the pastures into the forest, taking the path to the spot where she met Vusi the day before. When they parted yesterday, giving each other shy smiles, they had no arrangement to meet again. They didn't know enough of each other's language, if nothing else. But Shirley hopes the boy will come along the same path again today.

She sits on a smooth rock in a shady clearing on the path, surrounded by rustling trees, well out of sight of the house. She opens a notebook and stares at the blank page—she is supposed to write an essay for an English class tomorrow but doodles with her pen, unable to concentrate. When she grows tired of drawing, she tears a page from the notebook and folds it into a paper airplane. She is very proud of her paper airplanes; no one in her class at school can beat them for distance or flight duration.

She tosses her plane into the air and watches it dip and soar, then dive past an ancient Natal mahogany tree that stands on the edge of the clearing.

The paper plane arrives at the same time as Vusi and Gillette, and it strikes the boy on the head.

"*Hau!*" he shouts in surprise, fearing this strange white dart is the work of evil spirits. He is about to turn and run, when he catches sight of Shirley.

"Sorry!" she gasps, overjoyed that he is here. "I didn't know you were coming. I mean I hoped you were coming, but not at that moment. Otherwise I would have been more careful. But I mean I'm glad you've come . . ." Shirley realizes she is babbling and that Vusi doesn't understand a word she is saying.

He picks up the dart and looks at it quizzically. He sees it is a harmless piece of paper that has been folded in a complicated way.

"Here, let me show you." Shirley takes the plane and throws it into the breeze.

"*Hau!*" Vusi says again, smiling broadly as he watches it swoop up toward the tree canopy, stall, then glide in a graceful curve back to earth. He runs to pick it up, then throws it himself. But he uses too much force, and the plane dives straight down, its nose bending as it hits the ground at his feet. Gillette sniffs at it.

"Not so hard," Shirley says. "Like this. Into the wind." She flicks it into the air, more with her wrist than with her arm, and Vusi nods in understanding. This girl is clever.

After he has mastered the art of throwing the plane, he picks it up and tries to work out how it has been folded. He searches his head for the word he needs in English. He wishes he had paid more attention at school. Suddenly he remembers—it's the word that sounds like the Zulu expression for surprise.

"How?" he asks, holding up the folded paper. "How?"

Shirley motions him to sit on the rock next to her, and she tears another page from her notebook. Deftly she folds it down the middle, then makes folds to create wings and flaps to control flight direction.

She takes a new sheet of paper and gives it to Vusi. "You try."

But he is confused; she worked too quickly for him to be able to follow the sequence of folds.

"Look," she says, folding the paper for him, more

slowly this time. As they work together on the airplane, their hands brush together. Vusi notices her skin is much softer than his or his sisters' hands. Does she not have to hoe the vegetable patch for her mother? Does she never have to chop wood?

When they get bored with paper airplanes, Vusi reaches into his pocket for the present he has brought Shirley. He thrusts it out at her: a tiny bull modeled from river clay, painted black and deep red with shoe polish, bearing a set of horns made from big white acacia thorns.

Shirley gasps in delight. "For me?"

Vusi nods vigorously, smiling to see that she is pleased. He had not been sure if this girl would like his clay bull. In her culture, it might be an insult to give someone a miniature animal. White people were unfathomable; his granny had told him this many times.

Shirley stands the bull on her palm, holds it up in a ray of sun, and admires it from all sides. The head is slightly lifted, and the nostrils are flared; it looks as if it's about to charge. "It's beautiful. Beautiful!"

Vusi beams. He has never heard the word before, but it sounds like a compliment.

Then Shirley points at the tiny animal and asks: "How? How?"

She wants to learn how to make one! Vusi is thrilled. He will have a chance to show off to her. He leaps to his feet.

"Come," he says, using one of his few English words. "Come."

He leads them at a trot along a path that Shirley has seldom taken before, because it ends up at the bank of the Tugela, and her parents have told her the river is full of crocodiles. But the boy and his dog are so happy and confident, she feels no fear.

When they reach the river, Vusi pauses. He doesn't know this part of the Tugela—they are far from the places where he usually collects clay for his animal sculptures. He wishes he knew enough English to explain to Shirley that you couldn't use just any mud or the model would crack or crumble. She watches questioningly as he scans the riverbank. Vusi quickly spots a patch of dirt with the deep red color that signals good clay, drops to his knees, scoops a handful of the thick, sticky mud, and rolls it into cigar shapes, a thick, short one for the torso, thinner ones for the legs.

Shirley marvels as the clay takes shape under his fingers. In fifteen minutes the handful of mud has been transformed into a perfect horse. Vusi is pleased with it, but it lacks something—a tail and a mane. Normally he would stick pieces of real horsehair into the clay, but there is none around. He could use grass, but it dries quickly and doesn't look right. Then his eyes fasten on Gillette. Of course!

Vusi calls the dog and begins stroking him vigorously. As he strokes, loose hairs from the dog cling to Vusi's hand, stuck there by static electricity. Vusi carefully collects them and pushes them into the still-malleable clay, giving the horse a mane and a tail. The tail sticks straight out horizontally instead of drooping, but that can't be helped.

Shirley claps her hands in delight, laughing. Casually, she glances at her watch and goes rigid. It's one o'clock—the rest of the family will be sitting down for Sunday lunch, wondering where she is. She had thought it couldn't be later than eleven, but the morning has flown past.

"I have to go," she tells Vusi, jumping to her feet and pointing at her watch. "It's lunchtime, my parents will kill me for being so late." She pauses. "See you next Saturday?" Vusi looks blank. "Next Saturday?" she repeats. "Sat-ur-day?"

Vusi nods enthusiastically. Saturday he understands, but he's not sure about the rest of the sentence. "See . . . you . . . next . . . Saturday," he repeats slowly. "See . . . you . . . next . . . Saturday."

Shirley smiles, thinking he is confirming the meeting. But Vusi is just repeating the sentence so he can remember it and ask Mrs. Sithole tomorrow what it means. Shirley turns and runs home.

OVER THE FOLLOWING WEEKS Vusi and Shirley meet regularly, always far out of sight of the farmhouse, communicating in a rapidly improving mixture of English and Zulu. Vusi begins paying much more attention during English classes at school, and Shirley pesters Salome to help her learn Zulu. They find that despite their contrasting backgrounds, they have much in common. Both love to run, to splash in the river with Gillette, to explore new parts of the farm, to talk. They are fascinated by how different each other's lives are. Shirley has two wardrobes full of clothes, while Vusi's possessions fit into a small cardboard box. She can count eight close family members—aunts, uncles, cousins—but he loses count after twenty. She eats off fine porcelain with silver knives and forks; he eats from a tin plate with his fingers. There are three television sets in the Montgomery home—the Ngugu kraal doesn't even have electricity.

From the start, Shirley showers as much love on Gillette as Vusi does. Her heart goes out to the dog with the missing leg. She frets when Gillette swims far out into the river, in case he is not strong enough to get back to shore. When they come to a steep path up the mountainside, she picks Gillette up in her arms out of concern that he might not manage on his three legs.

At first Vusi is amused, but after a while he grows faintly irritated at the way Shirley treats Gillette. It is as if she thinks his disability makes him physically inferior, a cripple who cannot fend for himself. Gillette doesn't need anyone to make concessions for him.

So one day Vusi suggests a new variation on an old game.

"Let's play hide-and-seek. But this time Gillette must be the one that looks, and you or I must hide from him."

"Okay. But do you think he can do it?"

"Just watch. You stay here with him while I go and hide. Count to one hundred, then let him go, and follow him to see what he does."

Vusi jogs off into the bush, Gillette sitting expectantly at Shirley's side as she holds his collar. When she finishes counting, she releases him, expecting him to wander around confused. But he shoots off like a rocket, and she has to sprint to keep up.

Shirley's heart sinks in dismay when she sees where the path is taking them—a place at the river's edge where a tall tree has fallen in a storm, its top crashing down on the far bank, so the trunk forms a precarious forty-foot bridge across the torrent.

"Gillette, Gillette, stop!" she calls. If he tries to cross over the tree, he will slip and fall into the water, and they will never see him again.

But she is too late. By the time she gets to the tree, all she sees is Gillette disappearing off the far end of it and into the bush on the other side of the river. The bank rises sharply from the river, and Shirley watches openmouthed as Gillette leaps up the path like a mountain goat. Vusi steps out from behind an anthill at the top of the path, and Gillette rises on his one hind leg to place his paws on the boy's chest and lick his face.

WHEN SHIRLEY ARRIVES HOME that day, she is late for Sunday lunch again.

"Sorry, Mom. Sorry, Dad," she says as she slides onto her chair.

"Eat up, your food's getting cold," her mother says. "Why are you so late? What do you get up to all day out in the bush?"

"Oh, nothing." Shirley knows this doesn't sound convincing. "I like to do my homework in the open air. I take my books with me, I can concentrate better."

This is not a complete fabrication—she was trying to do homework on the day of the paper airplanes.

"Be careful out there," her father says. "You know there are leopards in the hills around here. And you never know when some Zulu is going to come trespassing. You should take Dingaan with you when you go off on your own."

Shirley has been waiting weeks for an opportunity to tell her parents about Vusi. It bothers her that she has had to keep their friendship a secret.

"You know, Mom, there are some black kids in my class at school."

"They're probably just as stupid as the ones in my class," her brother chips in.

"They're not stupid at all." Shirley scowls at him.

"Do they smell?" asks Charles, knowing this will infuriate her.

"What about them, dear, the black children?" asks her mother.

"Well, if I became friends with one of them, could I invite him home to play here on the farm? Invite him for a Christmas party or something?"

Henry erupts in a fit of violent coughing, his eyes bulging, his cheeks beet red. He slides his chair back and doubles over, and his right hand flies up to his mouth. He can't speak but gestures to his wife to pound him on the back. Dorothy jumps up to do it, and gradually he recovers.

"You . . . made me . . . choke," he tells Shirley accusingly, between wheezes. "I couldn't breathe." He drinks some water.

"It was just—just a question, Dad."

"Don't even think about it," her father says, wiping his mouth with the back of his hand. "It's bad enough that you have to go to school with them, because that's the law now. But there's no law that says you have to make friends with them."

"But Henry—"

"No *buts*, Dorothy. She's not bringing black children onto this farm."

"Some of them are nice, Dad."

Her father pulls himself up to his full height in his chair and glares at Shirley. "They're backward, Shirley, backward and superstitious. They believe in evil spirits, in magic potions, in witchcraft. They—they buy women with cattle. Can you believe it, in this day and age, if a Zulu wants to marry a girl, he gives her father a bunch of cattle, and then he owns her! How backward can you get? We have nothing in common with them. I don't want to hear any more about black friends."

Chapter

5

Gales of laughter echo off the trees, a man raises his voice to make himself heard as he delivers the punch line to a story, children squeal in excitement, the murmur of women's voices rises and falls. Walter and some of his extended family of brothers, uncles, aunts, sisters, in-laws, sons, daughters, nephews, nieces, and cousins are having Sunday lunch in the sunny clearing in the middle of the kraal. The gold mines around Johannesburg have closed for the Christmas holidays, and the thousands of Zulu men who work there have returned home, their pockets full of bonus pay.

One of Prudence's brothers, a miner, is visiting for the weekend, and he has brought a case of beer and a bag full of steak from the city. By three in the afternoon, all the steak is gone, most of the beer has been drunk, and the hubbub is rising to a peak.

Lindiwe and the twins are playing hopscotch with cousins from Pietermaritzburg. Vusi has disappeared into the bush with Gillette, as has become his habit in recent months.

Walter is telling his brother-in-law from Johannesburg about the cattle raid, three months ago now. The tale has become further embroidered. As Walter now tells it, the number of shots fired by the farmer has increased by two dozen; one of the bullets actually hit Walter, but the scar has disappeared already. The farmer sent his four Rottweilers after Walter and Petrus, and the men had to fight off the dogs with their spears. Prudence rolls her eyes at hearing the story yet again, then turns smiling to her neighbor to share some gossip.

As she turns, her smile fades; she freezes and falls silent. She puts her right hand on her husband's arm and shakes hard to get his attention. He looks around in irritation at the interruption, then follows her gaze and sees the yellow Mercedes. One by one the voices around the kraal are stilled. Even the children drop their game.

Every face in the kraal is focused on the car. Mouths full of food stop chewing. Arms raising glasses of beer halt in midair. The door of the car swings open. Slowly the driver steps out. It is a white man, tall and lean. By his wide-brimmed hat, his suntanned skin, his short pants, and his scuffed boots, everyone can tell he is a farmer.

The man walks around to the back of his car, opens the trunk, and reaches in to retrieve something. The raised trunk obscures the view from the kraal, but when he reemerges, he is cradling a heavy load in a black plastic trash bag.

The farmer approaches the silent gathering, his steps measured, his eyes squinting at the questioning faces.

He identifies Walter as the central figure of the kraal and stops ten yards in front of him. Holding Walter's eyes in his own, the farmer upends the bag so its load falls on the ground between them, landing with a thump.

Every face in the kraal is riveted by the sight. The stiff body of Charcoal lies in the dust, her blank eyes wide open, her rigid legs standing out from the torso.

"I think this is your dog, *madala*," the white man says in fluent Zulu.

WALTER TURNS TO PETRUS and mutters an instruction. The young Zulu rises from his seat and, watching the farmer warily, crosses to the dog's body. He lifts it by two legs and lugs it away to the deep pit where the Ngugus bury their trash.

"It's bad luck to have death in the middle of the kraal," Walter tells the white man.

"I'm sorry. But it's bad luck to lose your cattle, too."

The farmer has made the dramatic entry that he was seeking, and he has the full attention of everyone, but now he is as nervous as the Ngugu clan and their friends. Intimidated by the grim faces staring at him, the forbidding silence, he considers just climbing back in the Mercedes and driving off. Instead, he stretches out his right hand to Walter. "My name is Rudolph, Robert Rudolph. I own the farm over there." Robert inclines his head in the direction of his property. "I have come to talk."

His name is familiar to most of the Zulus. Has he come now to seek revenge for the theft of his cows, to make trouble? But then why does he come alone? Where is his gun?

Walter is not sure what to do now. Custom dictates that a stranger who comes in peace should be welcomed, given food and drink. But the kraal has never, ever hosted a white stranger before. And does this stranger come in peace? He says he wants to talk, but why did he bring the remains of Charcoal?

Walter rises to his feet. "I am Ngugu, Walter Ngugu." He stretches out his hand to take Robert's, and some of the tension eases. "Sit, sit," Walter says, indicating a thick tree trunk that serves as a bench. The men on the bench shuffle over to make room for Robert. There is an awkward pause, then someone offers him a tin mug filled with beer, and he begins to relax.

"We need rain," he says. A mutter of agreement circles the gathering.

"This drought is bad," Walter replies. "We have never seen the river so low."

The Zulus discuss the weather with their guest for several minutes more, and then the health of everyone in the kraal, and then the way prices keep rising, how hard it is to find work. They are patiently waiting for him to get back to the dog, to broach the real reason for his visit.

As Robert accepts a second mug of beer, he clears his throat and looks at Walter.

"I have an idea I want to discuss with you."

"We are listening."

Robert has been preparing for this moment for weeks, but he is not sure how to proceed. He gulps his beer and goes on.

"You are my neighbors, and I don't want to fight with my neighbors."

The kraal goes quiet again, and Robert feels every eye on him. He tenses.

"Three months ago, in September, a bad thing happened. Someone came to my farm, broke the fences, and stole a cow."

Robert ignores the stony silence. He has come this far, he will finish what he has to say. "I was very angry. Anyone would be. My emotions got the better of me, I took my gun, I fired some shots. It was the first time in my life I had shot at a person, a human being. Luckily, luckily, I couldn't see where I was shooting, and I missed. I missed the humans, but I killed a dog. I hope, I really hope, that was the last time I ever shoot at a person."

Robert takes another gulp of beer. "And I'm sorry about the dog. But I was still angry then. I wanted to find the people who had robbed me and make them pay. So I took the body of the dog and put it in a freezer, so I could go to the police and they could use it for evidence."

A low mutter greets these words. The stock-theft unit of the police is not welcome in Msinga.

"But then I thought about it, and I said to myself, okay, if I call the police, if they catch the man, or the men, maybe they will have to pay a fine. Say, fifty rand." Robert looks up at the faces around him, all listening intently. "But what would that help? What would it help? The man would pay the fine, he would become more bitter, and one week later he would steal another cow."

Walter gives a grunt of grudging agreement.

"So I thought, 'No, there must be a better way.' I asked lots of questions around the district, and I found out who owns a small black dog, a dog that looks different from most of the Zulu dogs. Because I wanted to meet the owners of that dog, I wanted to talk to them like one human being to another. I wanted to solve the problems we have."

"Tell me, how do you see these problems?" Walter asks.

"I have much land, with many animals, but you have little." Robert gestures to the landscape around them. "Your land is eroded, rocky. You cannot afford to buy cattle."

Walter nods in agreement. "So what do we do about it?"

Robert, encouraged, continues. "I want to share what I have with you. My idea is this: that you use my farm to hunt. That we arrange a day, perhaps two days, every month, when the people of this kraal come onto my property, with my permission, and hunt game. There is lots of game on my farm—antelope, hares, warthog, wild boar, lots. You will easily catch an impala or two." He sips the beer. "All I ask is that nobody touch my cattle."

Robert stops, his heartbeat pounding in his ears. Will these people just laugh at him? Will they tell him to go home and stop bothering them with jokes?

"What do you think?"

No one speaks. The silence extends into a minute, two minutes. Walter and the other Zulus exchange astonished looks. What their visitor has just suggested is so unexpected, so radical, they are not sure how to respond. After the decades of mistrust and hostility between whites and blacks in Msinga, why would this rich white farmer propose something like this? Walter is suspicious.

"Is this a trick? You want to get us on your farm, then call the police and tell them to arrest us because you have caught us red-handed, poaching in broad daylight?"

"No, no, no, *madala*, no. I give you my word." Robert holds his hand over his heart. "I want to do this for my sake, and for the sake of my children, and their children. There must be peace in this valley between us, but how can there be peace if on one side of the fence people are starving and on the other side there is plenty? The people with nothing will always be angry, hungry, they will always be bitter. Am I right?"

Robert and Walter hold each other's eyes as the Zulu tries to decide if the offer is sincere.

Suddenly Walter rises to his feet and stretches out his hand to Robert.

"Thank you, brother. We will do this together. Let us share the land of our birth."

Robert beams and pumps Walter's hand enthusiastically. "Look, next Saturday is Christmas Day, the day of peace and harmony. Let's have the first hunt the day after that, Sunday."

CHRISTMAS DAY IS LITTLE DIFFERENT from any other weekend day for the Ngugus. They have no extra cash to buy each other presents, and they do not go to church. The only sign of Christmas is a paper cutout decoration that Mandisa and Tendeka made at school, which they have strung up outside the children's hut.

Grandmother Ngugu gets up at dawn as usual and hobbles over to the kitchen, where she grumbles and rattles pots and pans.

For once, she is not the first one up. Vusi is in the kitchen before her, grinning from ear to ear as he stokes the fire for coffee. He cannot contain his joy.

"Granny! Granny! Guess what? Father is taking me hunting!" Vusi dances a jig around the kitchen, making mock spear thrusts, imitating the foot-stamping kicks of the stick-fighting dance. "We go tomorrow!"

His grandmother gives him a slow look of appraisal. "Yes, it is time" is all she says.

"Father told me yesterday, at dinner. I could hardly sleep!" Vusi skips out of the kitchen to go and tease his sisters, who are still in bed. How can anyone sleep on such a wonderful morning, a morning full of promise and expectation?

VUSI LEAVES THE KRAAL at noon to go and meet Shirley at their clearing. He knows she will be late, because she is going to church with her family, but he can't wait to tell her the news about the hunt. He whistles for Gillette, who sprints from the porcupine burrow that he has made his home. One fear nags at the back of Vusi's mind, despite his joy: going on the hunt tomorrow with Gillette means revealing the dog's existence to his mother.

Vusi waits an hour and a half in the clearing before Shirley arrives. He spends the time talking to Gillette and playing games with the antelope hide. "Tomorrow is your big day, boy. Tomorrow you will show the world that you are the best hunting dog in Msinga, that you don't need four legs! Look at me, I only have two legs. So already you are better off than me."

Gillette, fully grown now but still full of the playful instincts of adolescence, makes a grab for the strip of hide in Vusi's hand and darts off with it down the path that leads to Shirley's home.

Vusi gasps in fear: Where's the dog going? What if the farmer sees him? But then he relaxes when he hears Shirley's voice as she talks to the dog. Gillette had smelled or heard her coming and had run to greet her.

Vusi, brimming over with excitement at the news he has for Shirley about the hunt, doesn't notice how wan her smile is today; he doesn't see the sadness in her eyes.

"I have something very, very important to tell you," he blurts out. "The best thing that could happen . . . But first I have a present for you." Vusi reaches into his pocket and places the gift in Shirley's hand. "Happy Christmas!"

Shirley looks at the present—a perfect clay model of Gillette, with his own hair for a tail, and one back leg missing.

"It's to remind you of us when you go away to your school in Johannesburg," Vusi says.

Shirley sinks down onto a tree trunk, her elbows on her knees, her face in her hands, and breaks into tears.

Vusi is shocked. He has never seen Shirley cry before. He sinks down next to her on the log and puts his arm around her shoulders to comfort her, as he would if one of his sisters burst into tears.

"What is it, Shirley? What is it?"

"Oh, Vusi, I've never had such a miserable Christmas," Shirley weeps. She struggles to control the sobbing, tears streaking the dust on her face. "It's only—it's only five weeks before I have to leave. I'm so sad, Vusi, I'm so sad." Her shoulders heave, and she wipes her nose with a tissue.

"I don't want to leave my home, I don't want to leave the bush, I don't want to leave you and Gillette. Why are my parents being so cruel?" A new wave of sobbing overcomes her.

"But you'll come back, you won't be gone forever."

"It's going to seem like forever. I can't bear it." Shirley closes her swollen eyes and buries her face in her hands as if trying to close out the world. She hunches over with her elbows resting on her knees, crumpled like a puppet whose strings have been cut.

"You'll come home for holidays, you said."

"But I'll be gone for four months, then come home for only two weeks, and then I have to go back for another four months! It's awful, Vusi, awful." She leans closer to him for comfort. They sit without speaking, Vusi's arm still across Shirley's shoulders. Vusi doesn't know what he can say to console her. As Shirley's sobs gradually fade, she lifts her face from her hands. "But what was the news you wanted to tell me? Perhaps it'll cheer me up."

Vusi looks into her tear-streaked face. He feels guilty for feeling so happy when Shirley is so depressed. "Well," he says tentatively, "I'm going on my first hunt tomorrow. With Gillette."

"Oh!" Shirley is taken aback. She is about to say Vusi is too young to be hunting but stops herself. She knows that would hurt his feelings. Vusi has often talked to her about going hunting with Gillette one day, how this will be the ultimate test for the dog. She has never really given it much thought, regarding it as a dream of his that would be realized only after many years, if ever. She has seen Gillette tracking, seen him worrying the piece of old antelope skin that Vusi always carries, but she always thought of the dog's antics as playing. Now that a hunt is actually going to happen, as soon as tomorrow, she is unsure of her reaction. She finds it hard to visualize Vusi and Gillette chasing, catching, and killing a wild animal.

"What kind of animals will you hunt?"

"Oh, antelope, probably."

"What happens if you catch one? Will you kill it?"

"Of course! We will kill it and eat it." Vusi's guilt at his happiness is fast disappearing as he thinks about going out tomorrow with his father and the other men.

"Doesn't the antelope feel a lot of pain and fear? It must suffer terribly."

Vusi shrugs. "That is what the antelope has to do. It is the prey, that is its—its *job*, to be chased and eaten. Like a sheep."

THE NEXT DAY Robert sits on his porch with Henry Montgomery, waiting for the hunters. He takes a cautious sip from his hot coffee mug, feeling the caffeine drive off his early-morning drowsiness like the sun burning off the mist lying across the valley in front of them. This view always lifts his spirits, but Henry is scowling at the valley as if it harbored hordes of unseen enemies lying in ambush for them.

"You're crazy, Robert. I'm telling you, you're making a big mistake with this plan."

Robert sighs. He and Henry have farmed neighboring cattle ranches for more than twenty years and have seen eye-to-eye on most things, but not this. "Henry, it's worth a try. How long have we had this poaching problem now—ten years? twenty? And it's getting worse. We have to deal with the root of the problem."

"Well, we must just get tougher. They picked on you in September because they know you're soft. I haven't lost an animal to poachers for two years, because they know better than to try it with me. Don't just shoot the dogs—shoot the poachers themselves. Shoot to kill. That's what I say."

The small explosion of a teacup dropping and smashing on the wooden boards of the porch distracts them.

Henry turns to his daughter in irritation. "Shirley, don't be so clumsy. Get a cloth and clean up the mess, or get the maid to do it."

"Sorry, Dad. Sorry, Mr. Rudolph." Shirley disappears into the house, shuddering inwardly at what her father has said. She has come this morning to see the start of the hunt, hoping she might learn something that would help her share Vusi's excitement. She knows she cannot accompany the hunters, because it is a males-only pursuit. And if they did make a kill, she wouldn't want to be there to see it anyway.

Robert returns to the conversation. "South Africa is changing, Henry. You know you would never get away with that, with shooting someone for rustling your livestock. It doesn't matter that you're protecting your own property—you'd go to jail for a long time, and you'd lose your farm."

"I know the Zulus, Robert, and they're going to think that you're showing weakness. They're just going to take advantage of you. You know the history of this country—our great-grandfathers, and their fathers before them, conquered it by force."

"Force won't work anymore."

"It's still the only language they understand, Robert."

Robert sighs. "Well, I'm glad you've come today— perhaps what you see will change your mind. There has to be a way we can cooperate with the Zulus, for our own good. If we don't give them a share of what we've got, they'll just take it, sooner or later. They won't even need to use violence. You know how easily the government could create a law repossessing white-owned land?"

"Over my dead body," Henry grumbles. "Everyone forgets that we whites brought civilization to Africa, we worked for what we have today—we earned this land. We brought the railways, the roads, the gold mines. If it wasn't for us, the gold and coal and diamonds would all still be sitting in the ground, and this would still be a continent of peasants."

Robert is about to reply, but his German shepherd jumps to its feet barking, hackles raised. The two men look where the dog is pointing and see a small band of Zulus approaching, with half a dozen of their kraal dogs trailing behind.

"Kaffir dogs," Henry snorts. "Good-for-nothing mongrels. Look at them: skinny, flea-bitten, mangy. Probably all got rabies. They should be shot like vermin."

"Well, we'll soon see what they can do." Robert chains his dog to the porch and walks down to meet his visitors.

He and Walter greet each other like old friends.

"I hope today is the start of a new time of peace between the people of Msinga and the white farmers," Robert says. "I hope we can cooperate with each other and find a way to share the game of these valleys in a way that is fair and just."

"I hear you. We praise you for letting us hunt on

your farm. We do not want to act like thieves, like criminals. But we need to hunt, and the game is on the white farms. So this is the best way. We have one hunt every two weeks or so, we catch what we can, we leave your cattle alone, and everyone is content."

Robert and Walter shake hands again, but Henry hangs in the background, still scowling. Shirley watches from the porch.

"I think the best land to hunt is the northern part of the farm, where the trees are thin and it will be easier to see the game," Robert says, leading the way.

The Zulus fall in behind the two white men as they head toward a section of open savanna. Shakes has joined the hunt, with his two surviving dogs, Prudence's brother has come, and he has brought two friends. There are no women on the hunt, but Robert notices a young boy of about twelve or thirteen bringing up the rear.

"Isn't he too young to be hunting?" he asks Walter.

"No, he must start now. That is my youngest son, Vusi. This is his first hunt. He is just learning still. But his dog, I don't know. It has only three legs. I told him it is no good for hunting, but he refuses to get rid of it. Perhaps he'll learn today that he's wasting his time with it."

Robert looks again at the dog pacing smoothly at

the boy's heels and sees now that it is missing a back leg. Henry guffaws. "The dog's a bloody cripple! This is a joke. How can you bring a wretched animal like that on a hunt? It's just going to get in the way." Henry shakes his head, as if to say the boy and his dog have only confirmed all his opinions about blacks, and his conviction that Robert's idea is folly.

VUSI CATCHES SHIRLEY'S EYE as the hunters set off. They give each other a quick suppressed smile, but both know they cannot openly acknowledge their friendship in front of Shirley's father.

The boy can barely contain his excitement. All his short life he has heard the elders tell hunting stories, descriptions of legendary dogs that would find game every time they were taken out, and then have the stamina to stay with a fleeing antelope until it collapsed. Most of the hunts took place on the surrounding white-owned farms, so the men had to be constantly alert for armed farmers guarding their properties.

Now at last Vusi himself is out on a hunt, but he understands this one is different. The hunters have permission from the farmer, who wants to have good relations with the rural Zulus living around him. If all the farmers could be like this one, there would be no more night raids, no more shooting, no more bitterness.

Vusi is anxious about Gillette. When he left the kraal this morning with the other hunters, he could not hide from his mother the fact that he had been sheltering a pet dog against her wishes for nearly a year. She said nothing as she watched him go, but the way she stood with her hands on her hips, her face glowering in anger, has filled him with foreboding. The fury will grow inside her all day, he knows, and when he gets home, it will explode. She might demand that the dog be killed. She will say it is crippled and no good for anything, and that any food it receives is wasted. His father will not deign to get involved in a dispute over a dog; he has made it clear he considers a three-legged dog useless. If his mother says the dog must be killed, his father will shrug and agree.

The boy knows that the only way to save Gillette, the only way the dog will be accepted by his family, is for him to prove himself as a hunter. Today is do or die for Gillette, and the dog is hardly twelve months old.

Last night Vusi went to his grandmother's hut and asked her for spirit medicine, something that would ensure success for Gillette. She had given him a tiny vial filled with brown, musty powder.

"Jumping spider," she explained. "Dried and

crushed. Give it to your dog, and he will have the speed and cunning of the spider. Nothing escapes the jumping spider. His prey will be like the fly caught in the web, helpless, waiting to be eaten."

GILLETTE IS BEHAVING PERFECTLY on this first hunt today. He turned up his nose at the dried spider at first, but then Vusi mixed it in with porridge and gravy, and the dog gulped it down. Gillette keeps one eye on Vusi, watchful for his guidance, but lifts his nose periodically to read the information on the wind.

All the dogs seem to smell the first antelope simultaneously, turning as one and leaping over the tall grass toward a thorn tree fifty yards from the hunting party. The antelope, an impala, starts from its hiding place and bounds panic-stricken past the Zulus. As it leaps across the path, its swollen belly is plain to see.

Immediately Walter whistles to the dogs to come to heel.

"That one was pregnant," he explains to Robert, who is walking beside him. "We do not hunt pregnant animals. They must be left to breed, so there are more impala to hunt later."

Henry mumbles something inaudible.

"What's that you say?" Robert asks.

"Not bad, their dogs are not bad," Henry says with

grudging respect. "My Doberman would never listen to me if it was chasing a buck. Dingaan would just keep on running."

The hunters walk on, beginning to sweat as the midsummer sun climbs. They traverse the farm for two hours without flushing any further game. Most of the terrain is knee-high grass, but sometimes they have to push through thorn thickets that scratch their skin and tear at their clothes. The Zulus mutter among themselves. Petrus, walking near the back with Beauty, wonders aloud if a hex has been placed on the hunt. Robert is frowning because he knows this first day has to be auspicious if the Zulus are to accept his plan for organized, controlled hunting.

Vusi is at the back, as befits a young boy in Zulu society. He is tiring. Gillette's tongue is hanging far out of his mouth, and he is panting rhythmically, but his eyes are bright. Unlike most of the other dogs, his head is still up, alert. Suddenly Gillette's nose swings to the left, and he freezes, pointing off to the side of the trail, his nostrils working in excitement. Vusi has seen him act like this before—when he caught the rat at school.

The rest of the hunters and their dogs move on, not noticing Gillette's excitement. Vusi does not call after them because he is unsure what Gillette has scented. The adults would laugh at him if he called them back for a rat.

Gillette carefully, slowly moves forward. Vusi takes a firmer grip on the stick he is carrying. He hears a snort from the grass not ten yards away, then sees a blur of movement, and Gillette hurtles after the prey. The first Vusi sees of the animal is its tail, erect like a periscope on a submarine. Warthog! This is the most prized of the bush meats, tastier than impala, better than anything the butcher in town sells.

Now Vusi shouts to the others.

"Over here! Over here! Warthog!"

The other hunters look back and see the warthog disappearing into the bush, with Gillette bounding after it in arcing leaps that help him keep the animal in sight in the long grass. They send their dogs after them.

Half an hour later the hunters catch up to the dogs, who have cornered the warthog in a burrow dug into the bottom of a termite mound. The dogs know better than to follow the animal—it has small but razor-sharp tusks protruding from its bottom jaw that could disembowel a lion.

When the warthog has been dug from its hole and killed with the thrust of a spear, Walter takes his knife and hacks the two six-inch tusks out of the jaw.

"Vusi! These are for you," he says, turning his beaming face on his son. "What a hunter you are, boy! Today you became a man!"

Vusi clutches the bloody trophies, his cheeks too small to contain his smile. Gillette detected a warthog that all the other dogs missed. His father did not mention the dog when he praised him, but Vusi knows Gillette's position in the kraal must be assured now.

ON THE WAY BACK to the farmhouse, everyone except Henry is in high spirits. The hunting party walks jauntily, Robert and the Zulus joking and laughing together. The adults banter with Vusi good-naturedly, making him blush with pleasure. He notices a change in tone when his father and Petrus speak to him; he has taken part in his first hunt with honor, and he is no longer a child.

Henry walks behind the rest of the party, speaking only when he is spoken to. Silently he digests the day's events. Robert has taken a radical step by organizing this hunt, but what will it lead to?

They reach the farmhouse, and Henry takes his leave. "Well, Robert, for better or worse, I think you've started something today with this hunt."

Robert can hardly contain his happiness. "It went

well, didn't it? I tell you, this is the beginning of a whole new relationship with the Zulus."

"I'm not so sure about that. If I know the Zulus, give them an inch, and they'll try to take a mile." Henry gets into his BMW and starts the engine.

"Oh, don't be such a pessimist," Robert replies. "We must have one of these hunts on your farm next."

"That'll be the day," Henry snorts, and drives off.

ROBERT GIVES THE HUNTING PARTY a ride back to the Ngugu kraal in his pickup truck. Walter and Shakes squeeze into the cab with Robert, and the others sit in back with the dogs and the warthog carcass. On the way they pass around a jug of beer and sing hunting songs, singing louder and louder as the level of beer drops in the jug. With one hand Vusi hugs Gillette, with the other he bangs on the side of the truck in time with the singing. He cannot remember a happier day in his life.

The truck arrives outside the kraal, and the men clamber out. Robert shakes hands all around and rubs Vusi's curly head affectionately. "That's a good dog you have there. Don't let anyone tell you otherwise."

The pickup truck pulls off, and the hunters walk toward the huts. Vusi is expecting his sisters to come running, to find out what happened on the hunt, but there is no sign of them. The kraal seems deserted, as if a plague has swept through in their absence.

Then Vusi sees the figure of his mother step out from the dark kitchen doorway and advance toward them. Anger shines from her eyes, her teeth are clenched, and she holds the heavy wood-chopping ax firmly in both hands, ready to swing. As he had feared, his mother must have spent the day brooding about Gillette, about how he, Vusi, had defied her. Her resentment has built up like hot magma trapped in a volcano, and now she is ready to erupt.

"Walter!" she shouts at her husband. "Are you going to kill that dog, or must I?"

Vusi drops to the ground next to Gillette and throws both arms around him. This can't be happening, not after the dog proved himself on the hunt today. He glances around, to see if he has an escape route. He would rather run away with Gillette, take him far from here where he will be safe, than allow him to be killed.

"Prudence, Prudence, Prudence, calm down," Walter says, holding up a hand in a conciliatory gesture.

"That dog must die now!"

"Wait, wait, wait. You don't know what happened today."

"All I know is that that boy has been fooling me for a year now. If you won't do it, then I will kill his dog myself, once and for all, and then I will deal with Vusi."

"Petrus! Bring the warthog," Walter calls.

Petrus and Prudence's brother have tied the front and back feet of the carcass together and suspended the beast from a pole. Grinning, they bring their prize up to Prudence.

"Look," says Walter. "Warthog. And Vusi's dog caught it."

The sight of the carcass silences Prudence. Her eyes swing from the meat, to Gillette and Vusi, then back to the meat. "It has been a long time since we ate warthog," she says slowly. Vusi holds his breath, watching to see if he is going to have to flee from the kraal with Gillette. His mother is thinking about how the warthog will taste. There is enough meat there to last a week. She cannot help herself; her mouth starts watering. She exhales with a sigh, and much of her anger seems to leave her. She relaxes her grip on the ax but still holds it.

"That dog, with three legs, caught this?"

"Yes, Prudence, he's a very clever dog," Walter assures her. "We were all surprised. We thought the dog was rubbish, that it was a waste of time to bring it on the hunt. But today it was the best dog of all of them. Am I right, Shakes?"

"Yes, yes, that's a very valuable dog. You cannot kill it. If you don't want it here, give it to me rather, I will take it. A dog like that, you don't find every day."

"But what about that boy?" Prudence asks Walter. "He disobeyed me, he deceived me."

"I will punish him, Prudence, don't worry. But we must let him keep the dog. We must be proud of both of them."

Vusi buries his face in Gillette's side to hide his glee. His father can impose the worst punishment imaginable on him, but it doesn't matter. All that matters is that Gillette is safe.

Vusi is still bubbling with excitement when he goes to the clearing the next day. Proudly he shows Shirley the two warthog tusks, which he has spent hours cleaning and rubbing so they shine like white shirts in a laundry detergent advertisement.

"My father says I must make little holes in them, then put them on a string so I can wear them around my neck like a real warrior."

Shirley smiles and pretends to show an interest in the trophies, but there is something about them that she does not like. They look like tiny elephant tusks, and they make her think of the men with automatic weapons who hunt down Africa's graceful giants and slaughter them for their ivory. Vusi holds out the warthog tusks to her, but she doesn't want to touch them.

"Why do you hunt?" she asks. "It seems so—so cruel."

Vusi is stunned.

"Why do I hunt? It's—it's just what Zulus do. If you are a man, you hunt. To be a real Zulu, like my father, like my brother Petrus, you hunt. If you are not a good hunter, then there's something wrong with you."

"But what about the animals you kill? Imagine how terrified they must feel while they are being chased, how horrible it must be for them to be stabbed with a spear, or shot."

"The animals were put on earth for us to eat. We *must* kill some, it's just—it's obvious. Don't white people hunt?"

"Yes, they do, but that doesn't mean I agree with it. I just think it's wrong." Shirley feels her cheeks burning. She has never disagreed with Vusi over anything before. "Can't you just go to the shop and buy steak if you want to eat meat?"

"Steak is very expensive."

Shirley is overcome by shame. Her family can afford to buy steak every day, if they want. Of course Vusi's family can't do that. If they eat steak once a month, it's a lot. She tries to smooth things over.

"You must be very proud of Gillette. My father told us he surprised everybody on the hunt by spotting the warthog." She strokes the dog's belly as it stretches in the sun.

"Yes, he's excellent." Vusi's smile has returned. "He's the hero of all Msinga today." Vusi is thinking about the hunt again. "You see, hunting is very important for us. My grandmother's stories are always about great warriors and great hunters. The very first Zulus were hunters, and we have to keep the old ways. We have always lived by hunting. You know, if a man is not a good hunter, he can't find a good wife."

Shirley doesn't want to talk about hunting anymore.

"Is it true that Zulu men buy their wives?" She blurts it out abruptly to change the subject. The idea has bothered her ever since her father cited it as an example of the backwardness of black people. She is sure her father made it up, and that Vusi will laugh and deny it. But he does not.

"Yes, of course we pay for our wives. We have to give the woman's father cattle, *lobola*. The better the woman is, the more cattle you have to pay. Don't whites do the same?"

Shirley is temporarily speechless. She always enjoyed comparing her life with Vusi's before, because they were learning more about each other and the differences didn't seem important—just a question of one family having more wealth than the other. But today she is discovering some of the differences are deeper.

"Of course we whites don't do that. That's buying and selling human beings, that's slavery! It makes the woman the possession of the man, like some—some *thing*, some *object*, like a car or a washing machine or a lawn mower!"

"Well, the man is the head of the homestead." Vusi is confused. He can't figure out why Shirley is so angry. *Lobola* is perfectly normal, he knows Zulu women certainly have no objection to it, in fact they would be insulted if a man courted them but balked at paying. His father paid *lobola* for his mother. Petrus is saving money already so when he finds a wife, he can pay *lobola* for her. Vusi fully expects to pay *lobola* himself one day.

Vusi thinks of a way to explain *lobola* that will make

Shirley see the logic of it. "If a man has to pay cattle for each wife, then if he is poor, he can only get one wife. So it stops a man from marrying more wives than he can afford."

He is quite proud of himself for explaining it so well.

On another day, Shirley might have made more of an effort to see *lobola* from Vusi's point of view, and she might have dismissed her inner revulsion at the concept as the result of the fact that they did not fully understand each other's language. She might have thought of *lobola* as a kind of dowry, except in reverse. But not today. She is miserable about going to boarding school, and Vusi seems to care more about hunting than her unhappiness. So what he says now only increases the emotional gap she feels growing between them.

"What!" she blurts out. "Zulu men marry more than one wife?"

Vusi realizes that somehow he has only made the situation worse. Shirley shifts farther away from him on the rock where they are sitting. Vusi wonders if he should try to explain further, but everything he says now just seems to get him deeper into trouble.

Gillette, who has been sleeping with one eye open,

jerks his head up at Shirley's movement. He stretches, shakes himself, and wags his tail. The signals are clear—he's had enough lying around in the sun for one morning, and he wants to be on the move.

"Oh, I completely forgot," Shirley says, glad to change the subject. She wants to talk about some safe topic, one where there is no risk of misunderstanding. "I brought Gillette a treat, a dog biscuit." She takes a bone-shaped biscuit out of her pocket and gives it to the dog, who crunches on it happily.

Vusi's eyebrows lift half an inch. "A dog biscuit? You mean a biscuit that is made for dogs?"

"Yes, of course. You must have seen them."

Vusi shakes his head in wonder. "*Hau.*"

"We give them to Dingaan all the time." Shirley always hesitates before saying the name in front of Vusi; she fears he might be insulted that her family has named their dog after a Zulu king. But he never shows any reaction. "Oh, I didn't tell you this—we learned he has a hip problem. He was having trouble climbing stairs, so we took him to the vet. It's still in the early stages, but the vet says it will get worse and worse until eventually he'll be in pain all the time, completely crippled."

"I'm sorry. That sounds like a terrible disease." Vusi pauses. "But tell me, what is a 'vet'?"

"A veterinarian, an animal doctor. You must have taken Gillette to a vet before?"

Vusi shakes his head. "Never. When the leopard hurt him, I took him to my granny. She's the only doctor."

"But what if he gets sick?"

Vusi shrugs. "I'll take him to my granny. She's very clever, she can fix anything. But she says our Zulu dogs are strong, because only the best ones survive. She told me if a dog is too sick when it's a puppy, it must just die. She says the Zulus have always done this, that's why we have no weak dogs now, because the weak ones all died long ago."

Shirley initially rebels at the callousness of the idea, but she remembers her father had said Dingaan's disease was passed from generation to generation. Maybe there was something to be said for the Zulu way.

"Let's move—I'm getting cold sitting here in the shade."

An idea is forming in Vusi's head about how to overcome the feeling of estrangement between himself and Shirley. "Let's go down to the river," he says. "I have a new way of making horses."

"What? What's the new way?" asks Shirley, her interest piqued.

"Wait and see."

———

Vusi nimbly molds the river clay into a horse about three inches at the shoulder and places it between himself and Shirley, suppressing a smile.

"That's the same as all your other horses," she says, disappointed.

"The difference is the hair." Vusi pulls out his pocket knife. "Take this, and cut some of the hair off my head."

"You must be joking."

"No, no, I'm serious, go on, it won't hurt. The knife is sharp."

Shirley looks doubtful but does as he asks. She hands him a palmful of his hair, which he takes and carefully pushes into the wet clay to form a curly black mane.

"Oh, clever! That looks wonderful!" says Shirley, smiling for the first time that morning. "But what about the tail?"

Vusi hesitates slightly. "I thought it would look good with a straight white tail."

It slowly dawns on Shirley what he means. "Of course! What a great idea. Here, take the knife and cut some off."

Vusi saws through a short lock of Shirley's long blond hair and pushes it into the clay. The hair falls to behind the knee of the model horse like a real tail.

"It's perfect! That's beautiful!"

"You have this one," says Vusi. "Now I'll make another one for myself."

WHEN VUSI ARRIVES HOME with his horse with the curly black mane and the straight white tail, he goes straight to his grandmother's hut. He kneels respectfully outside the door and whispers urgently: "Grandmother! Grandmother! Can I come in?"

An arthritic hand pulls the curtain aside. "Come in, boy, come in. You haven't been to see me for weeks. I thought you'd forgotten me." Each time he sees her, Vusi thinks his grandmother has shrunk another inch and is curled over another degree or two.

He sits just inside the entrance, staring at the dirt floor of the hut so he doesn't have to look at his grandmother's collection of horrors. "Granny, I need a favor."

"A favor. Well, that's what I do, I try to help people with their problems. What favor?"

"There is a girl."

"*Hau!* So young, and in trouble with girls already! They are always trouble, always, always, always."

Vusi sighs. "This girl used to like me, I know. But today she was different. It was as if when I said something, she did not hear what I actually said, but heard something else, something I did not mean."

"Yes, yes, that is quite common. It could be one of the ancestors, playing tricks, whispering in her ear to confuse her. Did you feel there was something like an invisible curtain between you?"

"Exactly, Granny, yes. We were close together, but she seemed so far away." Vusi's face crumples as he talks about it. "Granny, can you help me? Can you make this girl like me again?"

"Oh, this is what I do all the time, all the time. But I need something belonging to this girl, something very personal of hers."

"I have something, Granny." Vusi gives his grandmother the model horse. "The tail is a piece of her hair."

His grandmother takes the horse and looks at the lock of Shirley's hair, then does a double take and holds the horse's tail closer to her face. "I see so badly now, this looks like a white girl's hair! My eyes are playing tricks on me."

"She is a white girl, Granny."

"*Hau!* A white girl! Now that is really trouble." The old woman mutters to herself in worried tones.

"But you will still help me, Granny?"

She mutters some more, fingering the soft blond hair.

"Why are you talking to white girls? What's wrong with Zulus?" But she hushes him when he tries to answer. "Yes," she says finally. "I will try to help. But I don't know if my power works on white people." She tugs the tail out of the clay horse and clasps it tightly in her hand, closing her eyes and concentrating as though she were listening for a message from the hair.

"I will ask the ancestors to send her dreams about you. Very powerful dreams, that will make her fall in love with you."

"I just want her to be my friend again, Granny."

"Go now, boy, go. I must be alone."

"Thank you, Granny, thank you." Vusi ducks backward out of the doorway gratefully, taking a deep breath of fresh air. He realizes he hardly breathed at all while he was in the hut because he was so scared of inhaling some malign essence along with the room's pungent smells.

SHIRLEY FOLLOWS VUSI along a familiar winding path through the bush, listening to the morning birds calling and singing, enjoying the patterns of sunlight falling through the canopy of leaves.

"How much farther?" she shouts ahead. She is getting thirsty.

"Not much farther," he replies, increasing his pace. "Follow me."

They come out of the trees, and Shirley looks up at the clouds, swirling in fast patterns as the high-altitude winds push them on some urgent mission in the west.

"The clouds look like armies charging off to war," she says, but Vusi appears not to hear her. Steady thunder roars in her ears as if a fleet of heavy planes were flying overhead.

Shirley looks down and freezes in terror.

Vusi has led them onto the tree trunk over the river, the one she saw Gillette cross with such agility many months before. The din she hears is the muddy brown water rushing past under their feet, about forty feet beneath them. The tree trunk is impossibly narrow. She wants to turn back, but without realizing it she has already walked twenty feet over the river, and it's as far to go back now as it is to go forward.

The trunk where she is standing curves dangerously, and she knows that if she moves, she will slip and plunge into the raging, foaming water below. Her body will be dashed upon the rocks and torn apart by crocodiles.

"Vusi!" she screams in panic and terror. "Vusi!"

He turns to face her, and smiles.

He has stuck the warthog tusks in his mouth, so he looks like a hideous monster, half man, half saber-tooth tiger.

SHIRLEY WAKES FROM THE NIGHTMARE sweating, her heart palpitating as if she has just run a hundred yards. She shakes herself to try to rid her mind of the tree-bridge and Vusi's leering image. She jumps out of bed and hurries to the bathroom to splash cold water over her face.

It's Saturday, and her usual routine is to have breakfast, then rush out to the clearing to meet Vusi. But today she walks to their meeting place slowly, the frightening dream still nagging at her mind, her departure for boarding school hanging over her.

Vusi is there when Shirley arrives. She decides to tell him about the nightmare—perhaps that will help to purge it from her memory.

"I had a dream about you last night."

Vusi's face lights up. "It worked!"

"What do you mean?" Shirley is startled by his response. "What worked? It was a nightmare."

"My granny's trick. It worked!" Vusi is so thrilled, he interrupts Shirley before she can describe the dream. If she dreamed about him, then they will be friends again, just as before, just as his grandmother had said would happen.

"What are you talking about? What trick?"

Vusi can't contain himself.

"You remember last time I used some of your hair to make tails for the clay horses?"

Shirley nods, puzzled.

"Well, I gave that piece of your hair to my granny and asked her to use it to make you like me again."

"To use it to make me like you . . . What on earth do you mean, Vusi?"

"Yes, she used your hair in a special way, she never tells anyone how. But she said you would have a dream about me, and then you would like me again." Vusi smiles, confident that the warmth has been restored to their friendship.

Shirley tries to understand what Vusi is saying. She doesn't know what he means about not liking him—she has always liked him, even last weekend. She was a bit shocked about the hunting and the *lobola* and the polygamy, that's all. But what is this about his granny using her hair?

"Is your granny some kind of witch?"

"She is a *sangoma*, a medium. She talks to the ancestors, and they talk to her. She is very clever—she can cast many, many spells."

"She used my hair to cast a spell on me?"

Vusi shrugs in embarrassment and looks down at his feet. He doesn't want to meet Shirley's eyes; they are beginning to burn with a pale blue fire. "Well, my granny does that a lot." Shirley's reaction is making Vusi worried. She doesn't sound friendly at all. If anything, the feeling of great distance between them is worse. "I mean, it's nothing unusual for her to make spells," he finishes, mumbling the words.

"It's like voodoo, isn't it? Does your granny make sacrifices? I bet she does." Shirley glares at Vusi. "My father was right—you *are* superstitious, you *do* believe in magic." Vusi tries to speak, but Shirley doesn't give him a chance. "And you tricked me! You pretended to want to make a pretty horse, but you just wanted to get hold of a piece of my hair! So your grandmother could use it in some witchcraft ritual!"

Shirley stares at him a second longer, then spins on her heel and runs back toward her home, pushing aside branches and leaping over fallen logs in her rush to get away.

"But it had to be secret, or it wouldn't work . . ."

Vusi is talking to her retreating back. She doesn't hear him.

CHAPTER
6

V usi! Why is that dog so fat?" Prudence Ngugu glares at her son.

Vusi has just returned home from school at the end of the day with Gillette trailing at his heels. His mother stands at the entrance to the kitchen hut, glowering at the dog.

"Look at him! He looks like a barrel!" Vusi's mother blows up her cheeks, spreads her ample shoulders, and curls her arms out at her sides to demonstrate the vast girth that she sees in Gillette.

In fact, the dog's ribs are just visible through the muscles of his torso, but Vusi has to admit to himself that Gillette is in much better shape physically than Spear, Lightning, or Beauty. He knows this is because he has been smuggling porridge and gravy out of the kitchen for the last twelve months, and his mother must now realize this is the most likely explanation.

"He is a good hunter, Mama. He catches lots of food for himself. Lots of rats. That is why we never see rats around the kraal anymore."

This is at least partly true. Gillette does catch lots of rats. But he never eats them—just shakes them to kill them, then drops them for the ants to swarm over and reduce to fragile bones.

Prudence snorts in disbelief but turns back into the kitchen without saying anything more. After the hunt on Robert's farm, Gillette ended his exile in the bush and now lives openly in the kraal. But Vusi's mother accepts his presence only under protest, still smarting from the fact that her son defied her in keeping the dog and deceived her by keeping it secret.

Her irritation over Gillette is fed by a deeper anxiety, one that has been growing in the months since the men in the BMW fired at her husband's taxi and made him crash. Walter has not been shot at again, but sometimes he sees the BMW tailing him as he makes the run to Pietermaritzburg and back. Some of his fellow drivers have been intimidated by armed gangsters into abandoning the route, and Prudence wishes her husband would do the same.

Every day now when she begins preparing the evening meal, she worries. Will Walter come home to share their dinner tonight? Or is today the day the gangsters attack? Is his taxi even now lying on its side at the edge of the road? Is Walter injured? Is he dead?

She tries to drive the thoughts from her mind, but they keep returning. She turns on the radio, hoping for music, for distraction. But it is the news.

"... *the minister of safety and security issued a statement after the attack, saying he would order police to crack down on the taxi operators behind the violence. The attack today, in which four people were killed and seven were wounded, takes the total death toll ...*"

Prudence stifles the scream that is forming in her throat. Has it happened? Is Walter dead?

"... *in taxi violence to seventeen since the beginning of the year. To recap that story, masked gunmen armed with AK-47 rifles have attacked a crowded taxi rank in Johannesburg, the third such attack in January.*"

Prudence sinks onto a chair, breathing deeply, her panic easing. The attack was hundreds of miles away. This time Walter was not the victim. But she thinks, with so many guns in the country, left over from southern Africa's decades of guerrilla war, and with so many ruthless men prepared to use them, it can only be a matter of time for Walter.

It grows dark. The food is ready. Prudence has no watch, but she knows Walter should be home by now. She sweeps the kitchen floor for the third time since lunch. She brings in more wood for the cooking stove, although the pile of wood on the kitchen floor is already so high, it is in danger of toppling over. Impatiently she turns off the bright dance music on the radio. Vusi, Lindiwe, Tendeka, and Mandisa wait fearfully in their hut for their mother to call them to come to eat. They always wait for their father to return before they start dinner, and when he is late, like tonight, they know better than to provoke their mother by telling her how hungry they are.

Prudence steps out of the kitchen and walks toward the approach road to the kraal. The dogs slink out of her way. She stares down the road but sees only the night. She waits ten minutes, but then her shoulders slump, her head drops, and she turns back to the kraal. She enters the hut she shares with her husband, slams the door behind her, drops onto the bed, and heaves a deep sigh of anguish.

As the first tears run down her cheeks, she hears the engine of the Toyota van approach in the distance.

———

WALTER CLIMBS WEARILY out of the van and slams the door closed with more force than necessary. His wife runs to greet him, torn between anger that he has caused her so much worry and relief that he is not injured, not dead by the side of the road. She flings her arms around him and sobs into his chest.

"Why are you so late? I thought they had killed you."

Walter returns her hug and sighs.

"Is dinner ready? I had no time for lunch today. Let's eat."

They make their way to the kitchen, calling to the children that it is dinnertime. As she ladles out the food, Prudence returns to her question.

"What happened today? You have never been so late before."

The children eat quietly, their eyes on their plates. They sense a tension that does not encourage their usual teasing and joking.

"The gangsters from Pietermaritzburg stopped me."

Prudence feels all the fear come flooding back.

"What? What did they want? What did you do?"

"They blocked me with their car when I was leaving Pietermaritzburg on my way home. Four of them, all with guns. They told all my passengers to get out and walk."

Walter takes a mouthful of the beef stew and follows it with a gulp of beer. Prudence and the children stare at him wide-eyed.

"They told me it was my last chance. I must stop driving that route, or they will kill me."

"Did you tell the police?"

Walter snorts in derision. "Bah. The police will do nothing. They are probably taking money from the gangsters."

"So you must do what they say, Walter. You must leave that route."

"Then what? Then we starve."

"It's better to starve than be killed."

"Maybe this year I will find work," says Petrus. "Next week is the first of February—lots of businesses that closed for Christmas will reopen." No one replies: they know he is just trying to lighten the gloom, that his chances of finding work are as bad as they ever were. The family eats on in silence.

"I'm going to buy a gun," Walter says eventually. "Next time they come looking for me, I'll shoot first."

"A gun?" Prudence chokes in shock. "Don't be foolish. How can one man kill four? And if you did kill them all, there would be more. You know that. Forget this business about a gun. We will find some other way to get by."

"It's my route. I've been driving it for ten years. Nobody can make me stop. Petrus can come with me in the taxi every day, also with a gun. Then there will be two of us shooting."

Petrus nods. "Yes, we must fight back. I'm ready. I know someone in Pietermaritzburg who can sell us guns."

Vusi and Lindiwe exchange a glance filled with fear. This is a side of their father, and Petrus, they have never seen before. They know Walter as a friendly man who could be stern when they misbehaved but who never bore a grudge, who just wanted everyone to drink beer together and have a good time. This talk of guns, of killing, is foreign to their home.

Prudence says nothing more, knowing there is no point arguing with her husband when he is in this mood. Anything she says now will just make him more determined to confront his rivals. She clears up the plates and hopes he will think better of the gun idea after a good night's rest.

VUSI STRUGGLES TO GET TO SLEEP, and he can hear from her tossing and turning that Lindiwe is also still awake. The boy is disturbed by his father's talk of getting a gun, and he cannot stop thinking about Shirley. He has not seen her since the day he told her about his granny's attempt at sorcery with the lock of her hair. Two weekends now he has gone to their usual meeting place without her showing up. Each time he waited for hours, playing halfheartedly with Gillette, but in vain. Tomorrow is Saturday—he will go again. If she fails to come, he will leave a note for her, in case she visits the clearing one last time before leaving for boarding school. She will leave for Johannesburg in less than ten days. She can't possibly be planning to go without saying goodbye?

Vusi lies on his back, staring at the thatch roof. What will he say in the note? How about . . . how about if he asks his granny to make a potion that Shirley can give to her parents to make them change their minds about sending her to boarding school? Yes, he thinks, that's a good idea. Granny's last attempt only half worked—Shirley did at least dream about him, as she was supposed to—but that's no reason not to try again. Happy with his plan, Vusi drifts into sleep.

HE SEEMS TO HAVE BEEN ASLEEP only ten minutes when he is jerked awake by wild barking, strange voices shouting, and the piercing wail of a woman's fear. It sounds like his mother. Gillette is looking out from the entrance of the sleeping hut, his hackles raised. Lindiwe, Tendeka, and Mandisa are all sitting up in their beds, eyes wide in fright. Vusi leaps out of bed and goes to the door. The commotion is coming from his parents' hut.

"Come, Gillette, let's go." Vusi hurries across the kraal, turns the corner by the kitchen hut, and sees a tableau that chills his blood. His parents are standing just outside their hut in their pajamas. His mother is crying. Two strangers are facing them, smiling. But their smiles are evil, sneering. The men are dressed in smart jackets, well-pressed trousers, and shiny leather shoes, marking them as city people. One of them holds a pistol pointed at his parents. The other has a long, heavy stick in his right hand.

"Ngugu, you have been bad," the man with the gun says. "You were warned to stop driving the Pietermaritzburg route. But you ignored us. You are acting like a naughty child. You know what we do with naughty children? We beat them."

The two men laugh together.

"So my brother Joe here is going to give you a small beating."

Walter spits in the dirt at the feet of the man with the gun. Prudence steps between him and the man with the stick, screaming hysterically.

Gillette remains at Vusi's side, growling softly. The other kraal dogs bark frantically in a semicircle around the strangers. Lightning darts closer as if to bite. The man with the stick raises it threateningly, and the dog backs off, cowering. It knows the meaning of a raised stick. The man turns again toward Vusi's mother and father.

The boy knows he has to do something, now.

"Gillette, fetch!"

The dog leaps away from his side, reaching the man in three bounds. The man curses and lifts the stick again, as he did with Lightning, assuming this will be enough to drive off the animal. But Gillette knows from his games with Vusi that he has nothing to fear from sticks.

He launches himself into the air, clamps the stick in his jaws, pulls it from the grasp of the startled man, and runs back to Vusi. The boy disappears around the corner of the kitchen.

The man curses and runs after Gillette to retrieve his stick. As he rounds the corner of the kitchen hut, Vusi, waiting there in ambush, sticks out his foot. The man trips, falling headlong onto the hard ground. The boy takes the stick from Gillette and desperately beats at the man's head with it.

"Bite him, Gillette, bite him!"

The dog has never bitten a human before. He looks up at Vusi. He doesn't know this command, "Bite him."

The man rises to his knees, fending off the blows from Vusi. The boy is frantic. Why doesn't Gillette help him? Why doesn't he bite?

"Gillette!" he screams in panic. A jolt of adrenaline clears Vusi's racing mind.

"Geddit!" he yells, feigning a grab for the man's jacket. Immediately the dog leaps in, gripping the thick cloth and pulling the man off balance. Now Gillette understands the game. It's tug-of-war time. He must treat this man's clothes like his thong of antelope hide—he must bite and not let go.

Gillette's excitement communicates itself to the other dogs, who quickly join the frenzy. The man is panicking, flailing at the dogs, but this just heightens their excitement. They tear great holes in the man's clothes, drawing blood from his arms, wrists, and legs. He yells in pain as Beauty sinks her fangs into his ankle.

In front of the hut, the man with the gun hears the commotion. "Joe! Joe! What's going on there?"

"Help me! Come shoot these dogs! Quickly, quickly!"

The man hesitates, then takes his eyes off Walter as he turns to help his partner. Walter grabs his chance. He throws himself at the gunman and with his overpowering bulk sends him crashing to the ground. The pistol falls from his grasp, and Petrus, running from the shadows where he has been hiding, snatches it up.

THIRTY MINUTES LATER the two intruders have been gagged, tied hand and foot, and shut in an empty storage hut. Tomorrow Walter and Petrus will take them to the police at Tugela Ferry.

Vusi is about to return to bed. "Goodnight, Father. Goodnight, Mother."

"Wait, Vusi," his mother says. "Where is that three-legged dog?"

What now? thinks Vusi.

"He is sleeping, Mama."

"Call him."

Vusi gives the short sharp whistle that would bring Gillette running from half a mile away. The dog appears almost at once, looking up expectantly at the boy.

"Wait," says Prudence, disappearing into the kitchen. She returns with a dish full of leftover beef.

"Good dog," she says, placing the bowl on the ground in front of Gillette. "Good dog."

As the dog gulps down the meat, Vusi is speechless. He gazes at his mother in surprise and relief.

CHAPTER

7

SATURDAYS ARE NORMALLY JOYOUS days at the Ngugu kraal: the children run around the homestead, free from school, Walter drives his last route at about noon, relatives from distant towns and cities often visit, and there is always a big meal in the evening with lots of beer, jokes, and talk that goes on until late in the night.

But today is different. Vusi sits with his back against the wall of a hut, shaded by the overhang of the thatch eaves. Gillette lies next to him, luxuriating in a tummy rub. The boy sings a litany of praise for the dog's role in overcoming the intruders last night. "Even my mother likes you now," he says.

But Vusi is still moping about Shirley. What seemed to be a good idea last night, to ask his granny to use her powers on her parents, looks in the full light of day to be fatally flawed. After her reaction to the hair episode—what did she call it, voodoo?—Shirley would never agree to have anything to do with more Zulu sorcery. Not even if it might mean she could stay in the valley and escape going to boarding school. Vusi decides not to even bother to go to the clearing this morning. He half hopes that Shirley does go and finds he is not there. That will show her what it's like to be rejected.

But apart from his own melancholy over Shirley, there is a wider pall of gloom hanging over the family. Petrus and Walter put the two intruders, still bound, into the taxi as soon as it was light and took them to Tugela Ferry, where they were handed over to the police.

But the elation that everyone felt the previous night when the two men were overpowered has dissipated today. Walter knows the victory is only a temporary one.

When the family sits down for an early lunch, no one wants to be the first to speak.

Walter, picking listlessly at his food, eventually breaks the silence.

"The gangsters have beaten me. I cannot drive anymore."

"But now the police have them."

"Yes, Prudence, but for how long? They were talking to us in the taxi on the way to Tugela Ferry, very cheeky, very full of themselves. They said they would be out on bail in a couple of days, and then they would come back. And when they do come back, they will not just try to beat me with a stick. They will kill me and anyone here who gets in their way. Even you, Prudence, even the children. They have no mercy."

"But what can we do, my husband? We cannot wait here for them to come and kill us." Prudence is relieved that Walter seems to have thought better of arming himself and Petrus, but their situation is still fraught with danger.

Walter pauses before answering. There is only one solution, and he does not like it.

"We must move from here. We must go to the city where I can find a job. I can work as a delivery driver, give up my taxi. Maybe Petrus will also get work. We have to leave here soon, tomorrow, Monday at the latest."

The children say nothing, but they are aghast. This is their home, where they were born and grew up. These hills, this valley, are all that they know. Their friends are here—here they can roam free. They may be poor, but they have fresh air, good water, and all the space they need. What will happen to them in the city? They have heard stories of how hard the life is there, nightmare tales of how people live in tiny shacks of corrugated iron, everyone sleeping in the same room, all the shacks jammed up against one another, how you have to walk miles to fetch water because there is no river like there is here in Msinga. You cannot find firewood. People in the city are unfriendly and rude, and there are thugs and gangsters everywhere.

"What about your mother?" Prudence asks. "She will not want to move from here."

Walter's reply is cut short by the hooting of a car outside.

Everyone tenses. Mandisa and Tendeka drop to the floor and cower under the table, hanging on to their mother's legs. Have the taxi gangsters returned already?

Walter rises and cautiously peers out the door. He recognizes the car and steps outside into the light, raising his hand in greeting.

"Oh, hullo, Robert, how are you?"

The white farmer approaches, and the two men shake hands warmly. Walter ushers the guest into the room, and the twins, shrieking with delight, teasing each other for having been so afraid seconds earlier, fetch a chair and a plate for him.

"I won't eat, thank you. Just a glass of beer, thank you."

They talk politely about the weather and ask after each other's health. Then Robert clears his throat.

"It's been three weeks since we hunted together and caught the warthog."

Walter nods, and Vusi smiles proudly. He glances out the door to where Gillette is lying sleeping in the sun.

"I want to celebrate the success of that day. Because we did more than catch a warthog that day, we started a process of getting to know each other better, after we had lived as strangers for so long. Even though we lived within a few miles of each other, we never knew each other. We mistrusted each other."

"Agreed," says Walter. "It's a good thing you did."

"So as I say, I want to celebrate. I'm having a barbecue this evening. I want you all to come and eat and drink with me and my wife, so we can cement our friendship. There will be lots of steak, porridge, beer, everything. And we must set a date for the next hunt."

Walter is lost for words. Amid all his troubles,

there is a ray of light. This white farmer, a son of the settlers who stole the land at gunpoint, a descendant of the invading soldiers who waged war on the Zulus, a man who has benefited from apartheid, is inviting the Ngugus to join him as equals at a family feast.

"Robert, Robert, Robert." Walter looks down at the table, trying to compose himself.

"I'm also trying to persuade my neighbor, Henry Montgomery, to come. You remember him from the hunt. He didn't like the idea of inviting black people onto our farms, but I think he might be changing his mind, slowly. I think we might have planted the seed of change in him."

Robert takes a gulp of beer, his enthusiasm building. "Just think, if we can persuade him, and then his neighbor, and then his neighbor's neighbor—soon this whole valley will join us. We can put an end to poaching. Everyone will live in peace together."

Walter smiles at his guest's eagerness. He looks Robert in the eye. "This is noble of you. We will be honored to come and eat with you."

Walter and Robert raise their beer glasses in a toast. Walter is smiling, but it is a tired smile, and Robert can sense the underlying sadness in the room.

"However, as for arranging another hunt—" Walter is about to explain that the whole family has to move, and there will be no more hunting, when everyone is stilled by a sudden sharp chirping that fills the room.

Robert starts in surprise, then reaches into his jacket pocket and removes his cell phone. "Sorry. I'd forgotten I had this with me." He holds it to his ear.

Walter knows what a cell phone is, but his wife and children have never seen one before. They stare in wonder as Robert talks into it.

As he talks, the farmer switches into English, which only Vusi understands, thanks to his friendship with Shirley. But everyone can tell Robert is worried. His voice turns sharp and agitated, and his smile becomes a frown.

"Bad news," he says in Zulu, putting the phone back into his pocket and rising from his chair. "That was my wife. She says the daughter of our neighbors, Henry and Dorothy, is missing. Shirley—she's only twelve or thirteen. She wasn't in her bed this morning. It seems she must have walked out of the house during the night, when everyone was asleep. No one has seen her today, and her parents are frantic with worry. They're asking everyone to help look for her."

Robert looks at the Ngugus helplessly. He had wanted this barbecue to be a joyous event, but now it seems it could be overtaken by tragedy. "So I must leave immediately. We might have to cancel the barbe-cue."

Walter rises to his feet. "Robert, we are real neigh-bors now. I must come with you to help you look." Robert steps up to Walter and gives him a silent hug, stretching his arms around the Zulu's massive girth.

"Petrus, you come, too," Walter says as they pre-pare to leave.

"And me, Father. I can also help." Vusi has listened to the exchange with mounting fear. Shirley missing in the bush? Anything could have happened to her.

"No, Vusi, this is a job for adults. Your mother and your sisters need you here to help look after the kraal."

Vusi knows his father is right, that there is danger now for their family. He is proud that his father thinks him mature enough to help protect his mother and sis-ters, but frustration fills him as he watches Robert's Mercedes accelerate away. Shirley needs him, needs Gillette. He cannot sit here doing nothing while she is in danger.

As soon as his mother returns to the kitchen hut, Vusi gives a low whistle and heads into the bush to-ward the Montgomery farm, Gillette loping at his side.

VUSI RUNS NONSTOP to the farm, slowing only as he nears the farmhouse. The gate is open because dozens of people are coming and going. Several groups of people stand around disconsolately, search parties that have gone out and returned empty-handed.

Vusi has never been here before: his games with Shirley have always taken them deep into the bush and far from her parents. Henry and Dorothy Montgomery do not even know their daughter is friends with a Zulu boy. He is not sure what kind of reception he will get, a strange black boy turning up uninvited with his dog in the midst of a crisis. He approaches from the back of the house, and as he passes a window, he hears a woman crying inside.

He recognizes the white man standing on the front porch from the hunt on the Rudolph farm. This is Shirley's father, the man who won't let his daughter play with Zulu boys. Vusi has always imagined him as an ogre, a fierce-eyed demon given to erupting in destructive anger, a man who could paralyze you with the force of his hatred.

But although he is burly, when Vusi looks at him now, he seems vulnerable, frightened, broken. He is frantic, one minute talking on his cell phone, the next giving instructions to the half dozen people milling around in front of the house. Shirley must still be missing. Vusi is glad to see that his father is not among the people around the house. He must be out searching already.

"Mr. Montgomery, sir. Mr. Montgomery." Vusi calls from outside the circle of friends and neighbors but cannot get his attention. The adults are all talking at once, much louder than he. The boy gathers his courage and wriggles between the men standing around Henry so he can pat the farmer's thick, muscled arm. "Mr. Montgomery."

"What?" He jerks his arm away irritably. "Go away, boy. Can't you see I'm busy?" Henry returns his attention to his cell phone.

"Please, sir. I can help, sir. I can help find Shirley."

The fact that the boy knows his daughter's name penetrates the farmer's anxiety. He looks at Vusi properly for the first time. "How do you know her name? Who are you?"

"I am Vusi, sir. I live just over there." He points toward the valley. "I know Shirley, sir. I can help to find her."

Vusi knows Henry probably speaks Zulu, like most white farmers of the district, but he uses English because he calculates the man will be more likely to take him seriously.

"You know Shirley, do you? How do you know her?" Henry hesitates, then shakes his head impatiently. "That's not important now. Well, if you think you can find her, go ahead. Go on, join the search."

"Sir, my dog will find her, using his nose. But we need something that has her smell on it, a shirt perhaps, or a shoe of hers."

Henry is forming the words to tell Vusi to stop wasting his time with this story about a tracker dog when he catches sight of Gillette.

"I know that three-legged dog. And I recognize you, too, now. You were on the hunt at Rudolph's place, weren't you? That's the dog that spotted the warthog." He pauses. "Okay. We'll bring you something of Shirley's."

Henry calls to Shirley's brother. "Charles, run and get a sock or something that Shirley's been wearing."

"Aw, Dad, you don't really think this boy's got any chance, do you? That's not a trained dog—that's just a mongrel from the kraal."

"Do as I say, Charles. If there's any chance at all that that dog can find Shirley, we're going to take it."

Charles, skepticism written all over his face, fetches a sock of Shirley's and hands it to Vusi, hesitantly, as though reluctant to give anything belonging to his family to this Zulu boy.

"Charles," Henry says, "I'm going with him. I'm sick of just waiting here hoping for news while everyone else does the hard work. I want to go out and search myself. I'll take a cell phone, but you stay here and coordinate things."

Henry hurries down the porch steps with Vusi and Gillette, adding over his shoulder: "Keep an eye on your mother, Charles. The doctor's with her, but still . . . Tell her we'll be back soon."

Vusi feels a tremor of nervousness at Henry's decision to join him but puts it aside. Finding Shirley is all that counts, and Gillette can do that no matter who comes with him. Vusi is eager to get going before Shirley's trail gets any older. "Let's play, Gillette, let's play!" Immediately the dog's tail stiffens, his ears pick up, and his eyes widen. It's time for a game.

"Where's Shirley? Where is she? Where is she?"

This is how they play hide-and-seek. Gillette knows what to do, but Vusi holds the sock in front of his nose just to make sure. "Seek, boy, seek!"

Gillette puts his nose to the ground and makes quick zigzags across the lawn in front of the house. Shirley's scent is everywhere, but the dog quickly finds where it is strongest and freshest. He leads Vusi and Henry off the lawn and across the pasture behind the house at a trot.

Gillette follows a straight line for five hundred yards, heading straight and sure through a gate in the security fence and into the trees where the bush begins. He waits there for Vusi and Henry to catch up.

Then he's off again, following a barely discernible path through the undergrowth.

"They've already searched along here," Henry grumbles. "How do you know that dog isn't just following a rabbit or something?"

Vusi knows it's better to say nothing and just follow Gillette. Only once does the dog hesitate, when the path broadens into a clearing. Vusi recognizes the spot: he and Shirley were here together once, just before their final meeting. Gillette seems confused, and Vusi realizes the dog must have picked up an older trail left by Shirley.

He holds the sock out for Gillette again. "Where's Shirley? Where is she?"

Gillette sniffs the air, first to the north, then around the compass to the south, then swings his nose back to the east, and dashes off with new enthusiasm.

Henry is sweating profusely. After following Gillette for forty-five minutes, he is beginning to wonder if they are on a wild-goose chase. Charles was probably right—this is just a kraal dog with no special talent.

"This path has already been searched today. She's not here. Are you sure this dog knows what it's doing?"

"Yes, sir. Gillette knows Shirley well, he can find her easily." The words are out before Vusi can stop himself.

"Knows her well? What do you mean? I doubt if Shirley has ever seen this dog in her life before."

Vusi realizes there's nothing for it but to tell the truth.

"Sir, me and Gillette play with Shirley often. Almost every weekend. Shirley is our friend, Mr. Montgomery."

Henry is stunned. He doesn't want to believe Shirley is friends with a black boy, but it could be true. Shirley does disappear for hours on end every weekend. She has always liked to roam the bush alone. A quiet child, somewhat withdrawn, it's quite possible that her secret life in the bush includes friendship with this Zulu.

"When I catch that girl—" Henry stops himself in midsentence. How could he think of punishing Shirley at a time like this, when she could be in all kinds of danger?

"Sir, Shirley has been very unhappy, about the boarding school." Vusi would never normally dare to talk frankly to an adult, and a white stranger at that, but their joint effort in this search makes the boy feel like they are partners and gives him courage.

"I know she was. She made it quite obvious." So this boy knows about the boarding school, too. Henry surprises himself by being willing to confide in Vusi. He may be black, but he's friends with his daughter, and he's helping her and her family in their hour of need. Maybe Vusi can throw light on why she left her bed in the middle of the night and walked out into the bush.

"I suppose her disappearance has something to do with the boarding school," Henry says.

Vusi nods. "She did not want to leave this valley."

"It was for her own good," Henry says defensively. "The local schools—" He realizes what he is about to say, that he does not want Shirley to have to go to school here with people like Vusi. "Well, we just thought it would be better for her to go to school in Johannesburg."

Vusi, watching the path for signs that Shirley came this way, sees something that turns his blood to ice. He stops to show Henry. "Look."

"Good God," the farmer mutters. "That's a leopard print, and it's fresh."

They press on with new urgency, fearful of what they might find. If Shirley did come this way, she is in trouble. Gillette suddenly picks up speed and sprints ahead with renewed energy. Vusi knows they must be close. The path here runs along the precipitous edge of a wide *donga*, an erosion canyon that falls about fifteen feet straight down on their left. The *donga*, created by rainwater washing down to join the Tugela, cuts an irregular scar for nearly half a mile through the bush.

Gillette stops in his tracks, so unexpectedly that Vusi nearly falls over him. The dog is peering over the edge of the *donga*, his tail curved stiffly in the air, every muscle quivering. Before Vusi can stop him, Gillette launches himself into midair and down into the canyon. He lands heavily on his hip, grunting as the wind is knocked out of him, but then he is on his feet and barking at the trees growing thickly on the far side of the *donga*, his hackles raised, his muzzle wrinkled in anger, his lips drawn back to expose his teeth.

Behind Gillette, Shirley is sitting on the ground, her back against the *donga* wall, her legs stretched out straight in front of her. Vusi sees that one ankle is badly swollen. She grasps a long stick in her hands, holding it like a sword.

Gillette's barking grows more frenzied, and then Vusi and Henry see it: an adult leopard, almost invisible on the thick branch where it lies poised, perfectly camouflaged, its baleful yellow eyes fixed on the dog ten yards away.

"Shirley!" She lifts a tearstained face at her father's voice. "Are you okay?"

"Oh, Daddy, Daddy! Help me, please! Quickly! I can't move, I twisted my ankle, I can't stand on it, I can't walk, I can't get away. The leopard, Daddy, the leopard . . ."

Vusi and Henry exchange glances. They must get to Shirley, but the leopard is more than a match for all of them, even for Henry. It could go after them one by one if it wanted to. It is faster than they are, stronger, and it knows it.

Gillette darts toward the leopard, as if threatening to attack it.

"No, Gillette, no!" Vusi wails in terror. This leopard could kill Gillette with one swipe of its two-inch scimitar claws, pick up his body like a limp rack of spare ribs, and disappear into the bush, just like what happened to Sheba.

The leopard bares its fangs and in one fluid motion gathers its back legs under its belly to launch itself from the branch. It lands in a cloud of dust on the spot where Gillette was standing, but the dog has leaped away with a split second to spare. Gillette slowly backs off farther up the *donga*, still snarling and barking. The big cat crouches, staring at him, flicking the end of its tail from side to side in frustration and impatience. It pounces again, its claws arcing through the air, missing the dog by inches. Gillette sprints away, up the slope and away from the river, dodging around a bend in the *donga* and out of sight. The leopard, oblivious to the humans now, leaps after him.

Vusi's first instinct is to follow Gillette, to save him from the leopard. But Henry grabs his shoulder. "Quick, while the leopard is chasing your dog, we must get Shirley."

He and Vusi find a spot where the *donga* wall slopes more gently and scramble down to Shirley. Her face is twisted in pain. As gently as possible, Henry and Vusi lift her back up to the path. Her father punches a number into his cell phone, then curses. "It won't work out here. I can't call in to tell them we've found you. Everyone's worried sick."

Vusi helps support Shirley as she gets a grip around her father's neck, and Henry hoists her onto his back to carry her home.

"What about you?" Henry asks, turning to Vusi. "You should come with us. It's dangerous for you to stay here, and there's not much you can do to help your dog now."

Vusi listens for Gillette's barking, for any sound that will tell him what is happening in the bush where dog and leopard have disappeared, but he hears only silence. He can't bear to leave his dog, but he knows Shirley's father is right.

If Gillette is to survive, he will have to rely on his own canine wisdom.

"I'll run to your house, to tell them everything is all right now. I think you will go slowly, carrying Shirley."

"Good lad," Henry says. "We'll see you at the house shortly."

Shirley smiles at Vusi through her tears, and his heart lifts despite his agony over Gillette.

HENRY WALKS SLOWLY, careful not to jolt Shirley. As Shirley clings tightly to his back, Henry thinks she has never seemed more precious. For the first time in his life, he doesn't know what to say. His first instinct is to blurt out some angry accusation, to yell at Shirley, make her feel guilty for causing her parents so much worry. But he can't make the words come. It struck him as he ran with Vusi behind Gillette that his daughter was becoming a stranger to him. She was spending the happiest hours of her life deep in the bush with a Zulu boy and could not share her happiness with her own family because he, Henry, had made clear he didn't want her to have black friends. How much more of a stranger would she become if she went to boarding school?

Shirley breaks into his thoughts. "I'm sorry, Dad, for running away. It was stupid."

"Thank God you're safe, darling, thank God. That's all that matters now."

"That leopard, if you hadn't come when you did . . ."

"It was all thanks to your friend Vusi and his dog. That dog is incredible—it followed your trail for miles. I'll never say another bad word about kraal dogs."

"What if the leopard has caught Gillette, Dad? If only I could walk, I'd help Vusi look for him."

"It's getting too late to go after Gillette now, but at dawn tomorrow I'll get Charles and some of the neighbors, and we'll all go to help Vusi look. I promise."

HENRY IS TIRING, his leg muscles aching, but he and Shirley still have more than a mile to go before they reach home. It will take another thirty minutes at the pace they are moving. He is visualizing collapsing in his favorite chair with a cold beer when to his relief he sees Charles and Robert Rudolph hurrying down the path toward them, carrying a makeshift stretcher made by fastening a blanket across two broomsticks.

"Vusi told us what happened," says Robert.

"Sounds like you had a close call, Shirley. I brought you some water, too—you must be dying of thirst."

Shirley drinks greedily from the water bottle and lies back on the stretcher as they continue on to the farmhouse, Henry and Robert carrying the poles.

Dorothy sees them from the porch as they pass through the security gate and runs to greet them.

"Shirley, Shirley darling, thank goodness you're safe, we were so worried . . ."

Shirley eases down to the ground from the stretcher, balances on her good leg, and throws her arms around her mother. "Mom, I thought I was going to die." She buries her face against her mother's body and gives in to her tears.

Dorothy holds her daughter tight, soothing her. "You're safe now, dear. I'll make you some tea and put you to bed. The doctor's here already."

"Wait." Henry rests his hand gently on his daughter's shoulder. "Before you go inside. Shirley, Dorothy— I've been thinking about the boarding school. Let's forget about it. It was a bad idea. Shirley, you must stay here with us, where you belong."

A GREAT WEIGHT LIFTS from Shirley's heart as her father speaks. The dread prospect of leaving her home, saying goodbye to Msinga, being separated from friends and family, has hung over her like a dark, heavy cloud for months. A broad smile breaks across her face.

Shirley releases her mother and looks around. Tottering on her one good leg, her arms wide, she calls to Vusi, shyly drinking lemonade in the background.

"Vusi, Vusi. Come closer please."

He approaches a few steps, bashful in front of the white adults.

"Closer."

He takes another step toward Shirley, and she embraces him, leaning on him for support.

"Thank you, thank you, Vusi. You and Gillette saved my life. I pray that Gillette is safe." Shirley puts her mouth close to Vusi's ear and whispers: "And I'm so sorry for the way I behaved these last weeks. I've been really cruel." She gives Vusi a final squeeze.

Dorothy helps Shirley up the porch steps, leaving Henry transfixed like a pillar of stone. He has just watched his daughter embrace a black boy. Twenty-four hours ago, if he had seen that happen, he would have lost his temper, he would have hit the boy, kicked the boy, knocked him down and stomped on him.

Now, though, he doesn't know what to do. The embrace was so heartfelt, so natural, so . . . *right*. He's confused.

"So they're just starting the barbecue over at Rudolph's place," he tells Vusi gruffly. "You'd better run along, or you'll miss all the food."

THREE HOURS LATER, as night closes in on the valley, Shirley is dozing fitfully in her bed, her sprained ankle packed in ice. The Ngugu family are at Robert's farm, where the warthog hunt barbecue has expanded to celebrate the safe return of Shirley. Vusi has never known so much back-slapping and hand-shaking. It is as if every person in the valley, man, woman, and child, white and black, has congratulated him. He keeps telling them, "It wasn't me, it was Gillette," but no one listens.

In fact, Vusi is the only one not in the party mood. He still does not know where Gillette is, and he has no appetite for the food. He is itching to go back to the kraal, because that is surely where the dog will return. If he returns. He asks his father if he can leave the barbecue early, but Walter says no, that would be rude. All Vusi can think of is the terror Gillette must have felt when he confronted the leopard, haunted by the memory of the attack in the porcupine burrow, the nearly fatal wound inflicted on his own leg.

A booming voice cuts through the hubbub of voices, English and Zulu.

"Where's the hero? Where's the smartest young man in Msinga? Where's Vusi?"

It's Henry Montgomery, just arrived at the barbecue after making sure Shirley is comfortable.

The crowd around the cooking fires parts to form a circle, and willing hands push Vusi into the middle. He stands shyly in front of Henry, the top of his head barely reaching the white farmer's chest.

"Come, Vusi, stand next to me." With a hand the size of a spade, Henry guides the boy around to his side, then leaves the hand on his shoulder.

Raising his voice so it carries across the valley and echoes off the distant cliffs, Henry begins his speech.

"Tonight I have come to honor someone who is young in years but old in wisdom and braver than any man here." A murmur of assent ripples through the listeners. Vusi stares at the ground, blushing furiously. "Today this young man, and his dog, did what dozens of men could not do. He found my daughter Shirley. She slipped into a *donga*, hit her head, and twisted an ankle. Others had searched along that same path and did not see her lying there."

Henry's voice cracks with emotion. The crisis is over, but it has left him in emotional turmoil. He owes his daughter's life to a Zulu boy. He has seen his daughter hug a black boy, and the world did not end.

"My daughter . . . my daughter was face to face with a leopard in that *donga*."

"*Hau!*" The audience is enjoying the story, because they know it has a happy ending.

"And then Gillette, the Zulu dog, found her. And do you know why the dog found her? It was not by luck. It was not by chance."

Henry waits a couple of seconds for effect.

"He found her because he knew Shirley, he knew her very well, he knew her scent. He found her because my daughter was friends with this young man"—Henry lifts Vusi's right arm in a salute—"and because they had been playing together for months."

A ripple of surprised comment rises from the crowd.

"I never knew about this friendship. I don't think any of us knew."

Henry waits for a denial from anyone in the audience, but he hears only murmurs of assent.

"The lesson that Shirley and Vusi have taught us is that nothing is as important as friendship. And that you can be friends even if your parents, and your grandparents and their grandparents before them, were enemies."

Another murmur of agreement meets his words.

"Vusi, you, with your dog, saved my daughter's life

today. So now I want to ask you, in front of these people, I want to ask you this: How can I repay you? What can I do to reward you? If it's within my power, I will do it. Speak, Vusi. What do you want?"

A silence falls on the gathering, broken only by the fat from the meat sizzling on the burning charcoal. Everyone waits to hear what Vusi will say. But Vusi is mute, silenced by despair. All he wants is to be reunited with Gillette, but the farmer cannot give him that. What else matters?

Then he remembers the radiant smile Shirley gave him, and the hug. The power of speech returns. He speaks in such a soft voice that those at the back can hardly hear him.

"Mr. Montgomery, sir, my family is in trouble. Bad men from Pietermaritzburg want to kill my father and take away his taxi. So now my father has no job, soon we will have no money, and we need a new place to live. You have a big farm. Do you have a place where we can live in safety, where the bad men will not find us?"

The farmer standing beside him is silent for a minute. He had imagined the boy would want money, a bicycle perhaps, maybe some new clothes, even a couple of cattle. This request takes him aback, but the more he thinks about it, the more he likes the idea.

This boy, in a couple of hours today, has shown him just how wrong he has been, how bigoted, how he has allowed his life to be embittered by racist hatred and prejudice. He has mistreated his black neighbors, his black employees. He has been unfair to them, he has made their lives miserable. He has soured the life of his own daughter.

Now, when Vusi asks his help, Henry sees a way of making reparations for the past, a way of making a new beginning.

"Of course. Of course! You are welcome to move to my land!" Henry beams with joy. The boy has come up with the perfect idea. "There is plenty of room on my farm. Where is your father? We must arrange this now, immediately."

VUSI LIES AWAKE tossing and turning, unable to fall asleep. In one way, the day could not have turned out better—he has restored his friendship with Shirley, and his family have been given a safe place to live and the promise of a steady income.

But he has lost Gillette.

He is tormented by visions of the leopard catching the dog, sinking his claws into Gillette's rump, breaking his spine with one bite. Vusi has seen the body of an impala hanging lifeless in the upper branches of a tall teak tree, having been carried there by a leopard. He imagines Gillette dangling like that now, like some carcass in a butcher's shop, crows darting in to steal bites of the flesh. He vows to himself that he will rise before dawn to start searching.

Eventually Vusi drifts into a troubled sleep. The night is warm, he feels feverish, thirsty. In his dreams, he longs for relief, an ice-cold glass of water, a refreshing plunge into the river. He dreams of ice cream, a treat he had once a long time ago on his birthday. His sister Lindiwe is pushing a cold, wet ice-cream cone into his face. Laughing, he tells her to stop, pulls his face away, and reaches out to push off the persistent cold, wet pressure against his cheek.

His hand closes around a dog's nose.

"Gillette!" Vusi is instantly fully awake, leaping out of bed and throwing his arms around the panting dog. "Gillette, you came back!"

Lindiwe and the twins jump out of bed, too, as excited as Vusi, and all four children light candles to search every square inch of the dog for wounds. He is scratched all over, but only by thorns. He outwitted the leopard, the most dangerous animal in the bush!

Vusi fetches water for Gillette, who drinks thirstily as if he has spent the day crossing the Sahara. Then Vusi lifts him onto the bed, where the dog falls asleep immediately. Vusi drifts off minutes later, whispering praises into the dog's ear.

THE NGUGU FAMILY MOVE the next day, knowing that the longer they delay, the greater the chance they will be attacked by the taxi gangsters. Henry has told Walter, Prudence, and Petrus that there will be work for all of them on his farm.

There is one problem. Henry has only one empty hut for the whole family to live in. Until the Ngugus have built new huts for themselves, they will have to cram in together in the single hut. Granny Ngugu stays at the kraal until her new hut is ready. Although she will be alone, she will be safe. No Zulu would dare harm a hair on her head, knowing she is protected by the ancestors.

As they unload their possessions that afternoon, trying to find space in the hut for beds, cupboards, cooking utensils, and all the odds and ends of everyday life, storm clouds roll in from the east, promising to break the drought that has gripped the valley for months.

Walter stands outside as the first drops of rain fall, his face stretched by the widest smile Prudence has ever seen on him.

"Rain! Look at the rain, Prudence! This is the best

omen we could have. The rain brings new life after the drought, and here we are, starting a new life."

Prudence smiles as her husband dances a jig in the rain, and tries to remember when last he looked so carefree.

The rain intensifies, big heavy drops that beat on the skin like a hail of gravel. Walter ends his dance with a flourish and steps inside. The children come running from all directions, giving up their games to seek shelter in the hut.

Vusi is the last in. Gillette is on his heels, soaked through. Ten yards from the hut doorway, he sees Prudence standing there and automatically veers away. He knows better than to try to creep into the same room as the big woman with the fierce eyes. The dog, tail hanging low, heads off to find shelter elsewhere.

"Vusi, where is that dog going?"

"To find a dry place, Mama."

Prudence snorts the way she does when one of her children has said something particularly foolish.

"Gillette cannot stay out in the rain! He belongs in here with us, with his family! Call him, child, call him!"

GLOSSARY

apartheid: literally, "apartness" in Afrikaans, the Dutch-based language of South Africa's early white settlers. It was an official policy of racial segregation introduced in 1948 which sought to keep white and black South Africans physically apart. Among other things, it barred interracial marriage. It was formally scrapped in 1994, when South Africa held its first election in which all races could vote for the national government.

dagga: marijuana.

donga: a gulley caused by erosion. *Dongas* are widespread in South Africa, and are often the result of overgrazing by livestock—because too much vegetation is removed, there are no roots to hold the soil in place and it washes away in a heavy rain.

kaffir (also spelled *kaffer*): pejorative term used by white South Africans to refer to blacks. Based on the Arabic word for "heathen," it is roughly equivalent to "nigger."

kierie: wooden stick of the kind often carried by Zulus and some other black tribes. Usually about four feet long, it is used in dancelike ritualized fighting, but is also often used as a weapon in anger. Many *kieries* have knobs on one end to make them more effective in clubbing an opponent. Some are intricately carved.

kraal: an African hut or collection of huts, often including a livestock corral. Kraals are built in rural settings, using mud packed on a framework of sticks and branches for the walls. The roofs are usually conical and made of thatch.

lobola: bride price paid by a man to his father-in-law. Usually paid in cattle.

madala: Zulu term of respect for an older man.

sangoma: a kind of spirit medium who is in touch with the dead. Sangomas are usually women, and use herbs and animal parts to treat sickness or try to influence events. Some claim to be able to make potions that will protect their clients against anything from bad luck to bullets.

The Africanis Society of Southern Africa is dedicated to conserving the type of dog represented by Gillette. More information about the society and the region's indigenous dogs can be obtained from The Secretary, Africanis Society of Southern Africa, 43 Malabor Street North, Lynwood Glen 0081, South Africa.